Some Strange Scent
of Death

❦

Some Strange Scent of Death

Angela J Elliott

Whittles Publishing

Published by
Whittles Publishing Limited,
Dunbeath Mains Cottages,
Dunbeath,
Caithness, KW6 6EY,
Scotland, UK
www.whittlespublishing.com

Typeset by
Samantha Barden

ISBN 1-904445-15-2

Printed and bound in Poland, EU

This novel is based on the true story of the Flannan Isles lighthouse tragedy, which occurred over 100 years ago. While every effort has been taken to present the facts and the characters in an historical light, some of the characters and events are entirely fictional.

My thanks go to the following: the National Archives of Scotland; Margaret H. King (Rev'd) who allowed me access to her records at the Signal Tower Museum, Arbroath; Cilla Jackson at the University of St Andrews Library for copies of the 1938 photos of Breascleit; Bella Bathurst, author of *The Lighthouse Stevensons*, who supplied a wonderful list of maritime books; Dr William Lam, lecturer at Ceolas for his emails on Highland music; Scotland's Lighthouse Museum at Kinnaird Head, Fraserburgh; Donald J. Macleod, who gave me the benefit of his local knowledge; Stephen Walters, a dear friend and maritime historian, without whom my knowledge of sailing would be sadly lacking; Alan Renton at the Penzance Lighthouse Museum; Merrilyn Macaulay, Breascleit local historian, whose breadth of knowledge and stories of old Lewis helped me create a way of life and a country lost to history, and Janet Nicholson at the *Stornoway Gazette*, Lewis, for the wonderful pictures of the Flannans taken by their photographer and for the cuttings of stories they've run on the disaster. Not to forget the *Highland News*, Inverness, which ran items on the missing men way back in 1900, and the Northern Lighthouse Board who preserved the records of that time so carefully and who deposited these records with the National Archives.

For the sake of consistency, the spelling of some names in the original documents has been altered to match those in the main body of the text. I am indebted to all who have given advice and assistance, but would stress that all interpretations presented and any errors that may be found are entirely my own.

A special thanks to Keith Whittles for the time given me to complete the story, and to editor Kate Blackadder.

Special thanks, love and light to Louis.

Last but not least, love and more thanks than I can conjure to Jacob.

We landed, and made fast the boat;
And climbed the track in single file
Each wishing we were afloat
On any sea, however far,
So it be far from Flannan Isle.
And still we seemed to climb and climb,
As though we'd lost all count of time,
And so must climb for evermore.
Yet, all too soon, we reached the door –
The black, sun-blistered lighthouse door,
That gaped for us ajar.
As, on the threshold, for a spell,
We paused, we seemed to breathe the smell
Of limewash and of tar.
Familiar as our daily breath,
As though 'twere some strange scent of death.

from *The Flannan Isle*
by Wilfrid Wilson Gibson

ST KILDA

JANUARY 1901

Murdo and his son Torquil descended the well-worn but dangerous path down the Oiseval peak, as they made their way towards Village Bay. The air was so cold it hurt to breathe, and the rain danced obliquely against the stacked cliffs below them. Here and there the grass tumbled over the edge in springy mats, the puffin burrows transforming the thin soil into a honeycomb. It was growing dark and twelve-year-old Torquil kept close to his father; so close he could smell the wool of Murdo's jacket as it dampened in the rain. The boy had one eye on the grey mass of Dún Island across the bay, as he and his father rounded the point. From this height the sea looked like broken glass, a thousand shards shattering the waters of the earth.

Murdo paused to get his breath back, bending over to rest his hands on his knees. Torquil placed a hand on his father's back and waited quietly for the wheezing to stop. While they stood like this the boy peered into the darkness below, where the sea crashed fiercely against the rocks. For a moment he saw nothing, but gradually it dawned on him that he was watching a bloated corpse caught against the rocks. It rose and fell in the wash of surf. Torquil left his father and lay down in the grass, paying no mind to the damp seeping through his clothes. Even though it was fairly dark he could see the dead body quite clearly.

'Pa, look.' Torquil pointed.

Murdo leant over the cliff. 'A man,' he wheezed. He grasped the topmost stone and with an automatic motion lowered himself down to the rocky shelf ten feet or so below.

'We've no rope, Pa. Come back.'

'I'll just get myself a better look-see, Tor. Stay there.'

'Pa.' Torquil wanted to go down the cliff himself; after all he was the one that had seen the body first.

'I said stay there.' The old man lowered himself again. A gannet took flight from its roost, screaming like a banshee as it wheeled above the cliffs.

'Are you alright?' Torquil leant right over to watch his father grip the rocks and twist round to clear the next shelf.

'Can you see it yet?' Torquil called. He wasn't afraid that his father would fall, only that he might be seized by one of his coughing fits.

'Aye. It's a man all right. His body's taken a beating against the rocks. But I'll no rescue him now. He's long dead

2

and he'll be heavy to haul up. If he's still here come morning we'll bring ropes. I'm coming up now.'

The old man's fingers found crevices Torquil couldn't see from the top. Surefooted, he climbed back to his son. By the time he reached the top he could barely speak.

'A man it is,' he gasped. 'A man in some kind of tweed suit. He's no from the island. He's too well dressed. We'll leave him be. Like I said we'll come look in the morning. If he's no here then the tide will have washed him away.'

Man and boy continued on their path to Village Bay. At first Torquil was upset about leaving the body overnight. If it was still there by morning then it would be cut to ribbons on the rocks, but as his father had said whoever the man was he wasn't from around these parts. Everyone knew enough not to fall from the cliffs. Their ancestors had lived here for over two thousand years. Knowledge of this island ran in their blood. If Torquil's father said this poor drowned soul was not from St Kilda then who was he to doubt this?

A curve of low-built houses hove into view. The boy shrugged. Perhaps the dead man had fallen from the deck of a ship, or off another island. He didn't know if there were any other islands in close proximity, but that could be it. That could be the answer, and with that Torquil dismissed all thoughts of the corpse. He'd seen dead men before. They washed up with the tide and they washed away again just as easily. It wasn't a regular occurrence, but it happened often enough that he could allow himself to forget about it.

ONE

∞

*J*oe dreamt that the cold Atlantic Ocean curled its bone-white breakers over him. He gripped his bedclothes tight in his fists and imagined he was holding onto someone by the sleeves, his fingers stiffening into claws. At any moment he thought he would be dragged to the bottom of the sea. The waves thundered inside his skull. Tossed by the surf, the depths took him and he felt the water fill his ears, nose and mouth – and then he was awake, his eyes wide and wild.

Confused for a moment, he tasted salt on his lips and thought he had been washed up on a beach, but it was only his own tears. He lay in his bed in the lighthouse shore station, crisp white linen sheets cocooning him like a shroud.

Outside the sea rose in great rolling waves to scour the coast. He could hear it now, catching the sound of his own breath between the hiss of each wave.

He fought to free himself from the bed covers. The thought of them as his winding sheet frightened him. He stretched in the cold morning light and trawled his mind for remnants of the dream, but it had already begun to fade; only the feeling of being drowned had stayed with him. He remembered fragments: that he'd thought the island was the only place left on earth. Not the Isle of Lewis, which seemed like the mainland compared to the island he'd been dreaming about, but Eilean Mor in the Flannan Isles where, almost exactly a year ago, the Northern Lighthouse Board had opened the new lighthouse.

Joe stretched some more and pulled open the curtain, staring blankly at the dark pattern of fields and sea. Away across the bay he could just make out the Isle of Ceabhagh and Eilean Chearstaigh, and the gentle mountains of Great Bernera beyond, and when he looked on them he also imagined the village of Calanais with its cemetery fronting the shore and a little inland the ancient standing stones; sentinels to another time. These last places he couldn't make out, but he knew they were there. He'd walked the avenue of monoliths that led to the stone circle many times since he'd arrived on Lewis. The locals ignored these stones, saying that there were just so many stones here who could tell which were holy and which not? Silently, Joe mouthed the Gaelic names of each landmark. They were only amorphous shapes in the darkness, but naming them gave him back a sense of control.

He was about to turn away from the window when three dark figures walking up from the shore caught his attention. Joe waited for his eyes to become accustomed to their movements, all the while trying to bring the figures into sharper focus. They hadn't come by the road, but across the machair, the fertile low-lying fields that skirted the sea hereabouts. When they were within two hundred yards of the shore station Joe realised he knew who they were, but couldn't quite believe his eyes. They looked like the keepers from the lighthouse. They were supposed to be on duty. He frowned and tried to make out their faces, but no matter how hard he screwed his eyes up it was impossible to see properly. He wondered why they were here. The relief steamer wasn't due for another five days. It couldn't have sailed to the lighthouse without calling at the Isle of Lewis first.

He tried to focus on the three men again, but they seemed no closer to the shore station than they were before, although they still walked steadily towards it. It was now that Joe had the awful feeling that he wasn't watching his fellow keepers approaching the shore station at all, but some ghostly apparition. He spread his hand on the windowpane to block the vision out, and felt his heart race.

'No, it cannae be,' he said, and closed his eyes for a moment. 'I must be asleep.'

He'd had these kinds of dreams before; the kind where he thought he'd woken up only to discover the world was even stranger, but this wasn't a dream and when he opened his eyes the men were still there, no closer and no further away. There was only one thing for it: he flung the bedroom door open and charged down the stairs. He was only wearing his long johns but it didn't seem important. He had to see for himself if the men were really there. He yanked the front door open and ran outside, not minding the cold rain that almost swept him off his feet. By the time he ran down the path and out into the road he was soaked through to the skin, his underwear sticking to his body, his hair plastered down, but it wasn't until gone some way that Joe realised there was no one there. He looked up and down, blinked water out of his eyes, jogged some distance in both directions, scared by what had happened and confused because there was no one on the road in either direction. It was still early and a few lights twinkled in the distance. The rain blurred the horizon and the pre-dawn light lent an ethereal glow to everything.

'No,' he muttered. 'Not forerunners. No.' He remembered his father telling him that old sailors used to say forerunners were the ghosts of men yet to die at sea. He shook his head. It would be hard to persuade anyone that he'd seen three dead men on the road, especially when those men were safely tucked up in the lighthouse. It was then that the cold hit him and he realised he was wet through. He turned back to the house, his muscles all atwitch with cold, depressed now that he knew he must indeed be mad.

Inside he closed the door quietly and stood for a moment in the hall, dripping water on the floor, and tried to get both his breath and senses under control. Feeling a presence, he glanced up the stairs and saw the little girl Annabella staring at him from between the banisters. She was the younger of the Principal Keeper's two daughters. Joe attempted a half-hearted smile. Annabella just stared. She wasn't scared. She liked Joe. He climbed the stairs and she watched him all the way to the top. He left wet footprints on each riser.

'Ma will tell you off,' she whispered to him as he entered his bedroom. Joe smiled again weakly.

'I'll say I'm sorry,' he whispered back, and he went inside the bedroom and closed the door.

Still shaking, he poured a little cold water from a jug on the dresser into the bowl he used for washing. Then he stared at himself in the mirror and saw his angular nose and black moustache topping his full lips. Here he was then: Joseph Moore, twenty-six years old, a Belfast lad originally, although he'd moved with his family to Kirkcaldy, in Fife, when he was twelve. He looked strong enough and full of life, yet when he held his hands out in front of him he couldn't keep them from shaking. He felt as if he was going mad, but who could he tell? Who could he confide in?

When he'd joined the Northern Lighthouse Board he'd been told it was a secure job and that they took care of their men, but he was also told about the discipline that came with tending the light. It was like being in a beneficent army. If you worked for the NLB you had to follow rules, be responsible and patient, have regular habits and know something about mechanics. Joe supposed the commissioners had seen a strong calm man they could depend on, someone people called a 'rock', and he thought he'd been chosen too because his father had briefly been a fisherman, at least that was what his mother had told him, and there was no better recommendation than to have the sea running through your veins. For sure it wasn't because he was either strong or calm. How could it be when he had to fight so hard to keep his emotions in check the whole time? He knew he was good at hiding secrets from people, at hiding his fears. He did it by adopting a series of routines known only to himself: counting, touching the stone he carried in his pocket, naming objects and places to make them his own and give him control. Only in this way could he manage his anxieties. Sometimes the routines would let him down. Sometimes he would feel the world dip away from him and his breath and heart race. When this happened he would suck in large draughts of air and close his eyes, waiting for the worst of it to pass. And now this: the worst nightmare he'd ever had, and he wasn't even sure it was a dream. He felt as if all the routines in the world wouldn't make it go away.

Joe stripped off his wet long johns and scrubbed himself dry with his towel. He felt a little calmer now, a little better. He sat naked on the edge of the bed and thought everything through, comparing the dream and the vision of the men on the road to other dreams he'd had. This time had been the most frightening of all, and yet he always had dreams about storms and drownings, or of men lost at sea and the world a boiling mass of water with a demon imperative to take him to its depths. Sometimes his fellow lighthouse keepers featured and other times he was alone; the last man alive. There were times when Joe thought that the bottom of the entire ocean was lined with black-eyed corpses, the awful truth of what lay await for him in the afterlife lost in the depths of their gaze. It was true that he was wary of looking at the darkened windows at night because he thought unseen forces were watching him.

He whispered: 'Perhaps this is what had happened. Perhaps I imagined the men outside because I'd had a bad dream. Perhaps I hadn't been properly awake after all, but sleepwalking somehow.' At least that's what he thought might have happened. He couldn't be sure and he certainly wished with all his heart that there was someone he could talk to. He'd tried talking to an itinerant cleric, a man the locals called 'The Missionary', because he thought that a religious man might be able to put things in perspective, but when he began it all sounded so implausible he couldn't continue. These things were a legacy of long-buried childhood imaginings come back to haunt him. He wanted to be rid of them, but believed they would stay with him forever. The dreams were one thing, but to begin to put his ever-anxious thoughts into words without anyone thinking he was mad, that scared him most of all.

I can't tell anyone. Not a soul.

He slid his arms into a clean shirt, and listened as the rain struck hard against the windowpane as if for the first time. What had he been thinking? The vision was probably all a trick of the weather. The storm had raged on and off now for days. If it blew itself out in time he would go on relief – they called it going 'off' – to the lighthouse in four days' time. If not then he would be stuck at the Big House, Taigh Mòr as the shore station was called in Gaelic, until the storm passed, which could be a week or more. That would take him into Christmas. With no wife or family to consider he wasn't really that bothered by the celebrations. It was good to eat ashore on Christmas Day, and the Principal Lighthouse Keeper's wife, Mrs Ducat, Mary as she liked him to call her, would prepare a spread that she would repeat all over again for her husband when he was relieved of his duty in January, but really Joe would rather be working. At the lighthouse he had the routine of the four-hourly watches, when he would have to wind the driving weights every half hour to keep the glass prisms revolving around the paraffin lamp – and those lamps had to be kept full of paraffin and everything clean.

He buttoned his collar and wished he was a different person altogether – someone who wasn't touched by the strangeness of life.

I don't want to be me, he thought. I could have been someone else.

*

Callum Robinson leant on the railings of the SS *Archtor* and watched the sea pass in great churning waves off the bow. His ticket across the Atlantic had been paid for by the Cosmopolitan Line Steamer Company, who had hopes of encouraging emigrants travelling to America to make the passage with them instead of the opposition. Cal was supposed to write a series of articles for the *Philadelphia Star* about life on a tramp steamer and for this he would rate a return passage to Scotland and a chance at a real story next time round. Fresh from writing obituaries, this trip was a step up for Cal, but it galled him slightly that his editor didn't trust him with news. He wanted to cover crime, of which there was more than enough in Philadelphia to keep an entire army of crime reporters up to their armpits in type, let alone the man Cal considered a complete ass, his editor Barnet Culpepper.

What did Culpepper know about Scotland? Nothing, that was what. Nothing. As far as Cal was concerned this trip was a total waste of time.

The ship had already been at sea for eight days and it hadn't been an easy passage. Even when the storm that had travelled with them calmed so that they could see the sky, faintly blue between the rain-laden clouds, the sea had remained swollen and heavy. The *Archtor* wasn't luxurious as steamers go. She was a merchant ship and carried few passengers, but she was comfortably fitted out and the worst Cal had experienced so far were a few days of sea-sickness, for which the obligatory 'jelly pot' had been supplied, although after downing a bottle of Scotch each morning for breakfast it was hard to tell whether he was just more drunk than usual. He drank because he was bored and nothing seemed to touch him. Nothing penetrated his thick skin. He rarely took offence at anything or anyone for longer than it took to down the next drink. That said, when a good story presented itself he would become a man obsessed.

Cal kicked the railings and cursed. He was supposed to have been allowed access to the bridge in order to interview the Captain and take notes intended for his articles. Yet so far on this voyage Captain Holman had only given him half-an hour during a lull in the weather. The Master of this ship didn't seem very amenable. Cal wanted to take the helm, to steer the vessel through the heaving Atlantic, and even though he knew that the likelihood of this happening was nil he had every intention of writing that the Captain had offered him the wheel as they steered a course around Cape Wrath. He had to give his readers something more exciting than endless trivia about the weather. They had to believe that crossing the Atlantic was a big adventure, even if Cal himself didn't think so.

The sea slowed the ship to a long roll and the clouds parted to show a clear dark night. Thousands of stars lit the black velvet sky. A more romantic man might have thought himself capable of reaching into that sky and plucking one of the pinpoints of light from it for his ladylove, but it was late in the evening and not only was Cal devoid of romance, he had no female companion and he was very drunk. This was not unusual and he didn't think that much of it, but to others it was sometimes a problem. Cal was liable to rant. He would repeat newspaper anecdotes to anyone that would listen so many times they would buy him a drink just to shut him up. Men took him for a louche Yank with no class and women were slightly afraid of him. Although Cal was still young, twenty-four years old, and quite handsome in a brooding kind of a way with his thick dark hair, regular features and tanned complexion, he did not generally go down well with the ladies.

'Hah,' he shouted out loud to the wind. 'Hah. Scotland on the starboard bow.' But it wasn't. It was the moonlight reflecting off the crest of a wave. The horizon dipped into the sea, the ship rolled and Cal was thrown off balance by the motion. He grabbed the rail and held tight. Wouldn't do to fall overboard. Wouldn't do at all. Perhaps now would be a good time to confront the Captain. Cal pulled away from the railings and staggered towards the steps leading up to the bridge. He fell against the first riser and cursed loudly. He'd long since mastered his own roll; it was the ship's he wasn't so sure of.

'Tell me Captain, what makes a good Master of a steamship?' Cal stepped onto the bridge and ignored the First Mate who tried to propel him back over the threshold. A warm damp smell hung in the darkened air as if there was something festering quietly in a corner waiting to be discovered.

'Excuse me, sir.' Cal directed his words to the man who had now grabbed him by the arm. 'I have an invitation to the bridge and I would be grateful if you would take your hands off me before I lose my temper.'

The Captain, a tall full-figured man standing behind the First Mate, nodded his assent.

'I find your men have few manners.' Cal smoothed his jacket. 'How long before we see this country of yours? I need to walk on dry land.' He wrinkled his nose and announced: 'This ship stinks.'

Captain Holman, ignoring the derogatory comment and avoiding the question, scratched his thick black beard and posed one of his own.

'Will we have the pleasure of your company on the return trip, Mr Robinson?'

'Well, to tell you the truth I don't know. I suppose I'll go home when I've finished my interviews.' Cal fished inside a pocket and pulled out his hip flask. He took a swig of the contents. The burning liquid fired his throat. It was the only sensation that really reminded him that he was alive. He offered the flask to Holman, hoping to share the one experience that still meant something to him; that of swallowing this luxurious life-giving tonic. Holman refused with a shake of his head.

'Now your crew can hold their liquor, which is more than can be said for that dumb ass you had me seated with at dinner this evening.'

'I don't have anything to do with the catering arrangements, Mr Robinson, and this isn't a cruise ship.'

'No. No, of course not. You're more on the…' and he sought for the right words. 'You're…. You know. The higher up the ladder you climb the less you have to do with the hired monkeys.' He took another swig and then ran a finger over the wheel as if it were a woman he was momentarily caressing before passing to more important business.

'Any chance of me steering this baby awhile?'

Holman squinted at him angrily.

'Sir, I believe you should remove yourself from my bridge forthwith.'

'Well now, you promised me an interview. And I got to see how this ship works or how am I going to report it back to the readers? You might want to be more accommodating Captain,' and Cal winked what he thought was a knowing eye.

Richard Holman, Master of the SS *Archtor*, turned his back on the newspaperman and peered out into the darkness beyond the bridge. The words he uttered next were tinged with sarcasm.

'Perhaps you'd like to take notes, Mr Robinson. Wouldn't want you to give your readers the wrong impression.'

Cal tapped his head. 'I keep it all up here. I have perfect recall you know. Perfect.'

Holman screwed his face into a grimace.

'We've been steering south-east by east at half speed for the last four hours. We're within range of the Flannans.'

'And they are?' Cal stumbled as the ship pitched into another wave and he fell against the wall behind him. This bloody ship. Sometimes he swore he didn't know which way was up.

The Captain, maintaining his stance beside the man at the helm, answered as if he were addressing a small boy.

'A group of small islands off the west coast of the Outer Hebrides. We should have the lighthouse in view by now.' He spoke to the man beside him. 'Have we sighted the light yet, Garnet?'

'No, sir,' came the reply.

Cal whirled round to look at Garnet. As he did so he dropped his flask. Its contents stained the deck a dark black, like old blood.

'Can't you keep this damned ship still for just one moment,' he cursed, bending to retrieve the flask, but falling against the Captain's legs. Strong hands reached down and hauled him upright. The flask was empty.

'Take Mr Robinson below, Macduff,' the Captain said. 'I think he's had enough of the bridge for one night.'

The man Macduff stepped forward and made to show Cal the way out, but the young newspaperman wasn't going to be put off so lightly.

'I won't be manhandled like this. I've a job to do you know and you are making it very difficult for me to do it. Your superior will hear of it.'

'Macduff,' Holman said wearily.

'Would you be coming with me now, sir,' asked Macduff politely.

'Not until I've seen these blessed islands your Captain's been spouting about. Eight days at sea and not a thing out here save the same bunch of dumb asses.' Saliva now flecked Cal's lips.

'What's our position now, Garnet?' Holman asked.

'We're within six miles of the lighthouse. She should be in sight, sir.'

They stood in the glowering dark trying to get a fix on the lighthouse. The horizon stared back at them blank on all sides; the firmament now shrouded with wisps of gossamer clouds, grey in the tomb-like night.

'So where the hell is it?' Holman shouted.

Cal came up beside him, clutching the compass with both hands and staring hard at it as if it held the answer to the missing beacon. He raised his bloodshot eyes to the distance and scanned the sea quickly.

'I could do with another drink,' he said at last, licking his lips and staring out of the bridge. There was nothing out there to show where the rocky islands were. Nothing at all save an expanse of water on all sides.

Holman said, 'Visibility good. No light from Flannan. Make a note, Garnet.'

In that moment Cal had the thought that they might never sight land again, and that being the case, when the ship ran dry of alcohol, he would die of thirst. He ventured a look at the Master.

'Are we lost at sea?'

'Hardly.' Holman turned once more to Garnet. 'Keep a lookout. We may sight it yet.'

'A missing lighthouse. Interesting.' mused Cal out loud. 'Is it serious?'

'Perhaps, perhaps not.'

'Like what?' Cal could sense a story. 'Tell me. What's happened here? Why can't we see the light?'

Holman sighed and turned away, but Cal pressed for more.

'Tell me,' he bellowed. 'Tell me what's happened.' He was like a small spoilt child. 'Give me something to go on, damn you.' He grabbed Holman by the arm. The Master of the ship gave Cal a withering look and addressed his speech to Macduff.

'Remove this gentleman from the bridge and show him to his quarters.' To Cal he said: 'Mr Robinson, perhaps we could talk in the morning. Goodnight.'

'Now look…' Cal began to say, but Holman motioned Macduff forward and the big sailor took Cal by the elbow and manhandled him off the bridge. Cal's protests were lost to the wind. Macduff was not a man to be trifled with.

Back in his tiny cabin the notion of the missing light stuck in Cal's mind. Why was Holman being so cagey? Were they lost at sea, or was it something far more sinister? If that was the case then there was a story to be routed out. Cal toasted this thought by opening a new bottle of whisky. He knew just the newspaperman to do it. There were questions he wanted to ask of someone in authority, but first he needed evidence. He would start noting down each lighthouse they passed from this point onwards until they reached Edinburgh. That would do it, he thought. That would do it.

TWO

MONDAY, 17TH DECEMBER 1900, ISLE OF LEWIS

'Why are you sitting on the wall, Joe?'

Annabella tippy-toed through the wet grass, which was longer by the wall, the fronds curling into the lichen-covered crevices. She leant over the top and folded her arms so that her head could rest on them. She looked up at Joe as he stared at the loch and he glanced down at her, placing a hand on her head, feeling the silky softness of her hair now damp from the morning's misty rain.

'I'm watching for the boats come back from fishing. I like to count them in.'

'Why?' Annabella jumped up and climbed the wall to sit next to him. He was her favourite keeper apart from her father.

'Because then I know the men are safe.'

'Why?' She was full of questions, this Annabella, with pearl-white skin and petal lips, eight years old and the brightest of the Ducat children.

'There was a storm last night and they took the boats out.'

'Pa says they don't go out in a storm.' She poked her fingers into a crack in the wall.

'Oh he does, does he?'

'Yes. He says the fishermen know the weather before God himself and that they wouldn't go out in a storm if you paid them all the gold in the world.'

Joe looked deep into Annabella's dark brown eyes and saw her father staring back at him. The Ducat strength showed in the lines of her face and her steady gaze.

'He surely knows a thing or two, does your Pa,' he said seriously.

'Yes, and do you know Pa saved a boy once that had been out swimming and nearly drowned?'

'I didn't know that.' It was a game they played.

'Shall I tell you?'

'If you want to.'

The little girl nodded and smiled. Joe was a good listener. He'd heard the tale a thousand times but he would listen to the child one more time, under the dampest of skies, the vast-motioned sea spread before him.

'Pa was out in the wee boat fishing offshore. An Italian man and his family had come to stay for a holiday and they'd borrowed a boat and taken it out to find a place to picnic. Imagine being an Italian! Well, this Italian man had his wee boy with him and they were rocking the boat,' and here Annabella rocked on the wall, back and forth, back and forth.

'And they rocked it too far and the boy went plonk, straight into the water.' She looked at Joe to make sure he was listening to her before carrying on.

'I don't know why they were rocking the boat. They just were. Of course Pa was in the water quick as a flash and pulled the boy up from the bottom. The wee laddie was as sick as anything. And the Italian was so grateful to my Pa for saving his boy's life that he gave him a violin, and that's the violin that's in the parlour. It says Cremona on it. Inside. It's a treasure it is.' Annabella beamed, looking mighty pleased with herself.

'Your Pa's a brave man,' Joe said, and he meant it. James Ducat had saved a boy's life. He'd saved that child from becoming one with the drowned black-eyed people Joe imagined lined the bottom of the ocean. It was more than he could bear to think about, and yet it was often all that he could bring to mind.

'I know,' said Annabella and she jumped off the wall, the lace on her petticoat catching on the stones and tearing slightly. It was fine lace, embroidered by unknown hands and now, here, it had torn. What did it mean? Joe's heart ached suddenly for the torn petticoat and the telling-off Annabella would receive later from her mother.

'Is it your turn to go to the lighthouse?' the girl asked coyly, stamping on some pebbles hidden in the grass.

'Aye. It is.' Joe sighed.

A tiny boat had rounded the point and was making heavy weather of the inshore current. He could almost see where the current divided and spun round the rocks, where the water became more placid; where its glassy stillness betrayed the tumult beyond.

'Don't you like the lighthouse?'

'Oh it's all right.'

'What then?'

Joe stared at this girl and didn't know what to tell her. How do you tell a child that nowhere is safe when your head's full of terrors and she is so innocent?

'There's a boat now.' He pointed, changing the subject. 'See?'

Annabella followed his finger to where the tiny bobbing shape fought the wind and the waves.

'I want to go to the lighthouse but Pa won't let me,' she said.

'I wouldn't either.'

'Why?'

'So full of whys, Missy Annabella.'

She lowered her lids and gave him a grin.

'Why, why, why,' she shouted, and twirled away from him, her arms outstretched. 'Pa let me climb the tower when we were on the Isle of Man.'

'That was different. You lived at the light with him. This one's out on an island. Just rocks.'

The tiny boat had passed out of view now. It must have tied up at the pier. Joe could almost smell the fish; almost see their still writhing bodies in the bottom of the boat.

'No, there's grass too. Pa said.'

'Aye there's grass. But puffins and gannets and guillemots live there too, and sometimes you can't see the grass for the birds.'

Joe squinted into the wind and tasted the rain's salty mist on his lips, felt the needle-pointed drops prick his skin like a million fine knives cutting into him. Would he bleed to death if the rain pierced his skin? Would it expose his heart, his soul?

'And there's houses there too,' little Annabella said.

'Houses too. But broken down ones. No one has lived there for years and years.'

'And there's a church. They must have liked living there to build a church.'

'Well, there's a chapel on the big island, Eilean Mor. But that's a ruin now. No one goes there. Most of the houses are on Eilean Tighe.'

'Where's that?'

'Nearby. It's another of the islands. There are fourteen of them.'

'Pa says they're called the Seven Hunters so there can't be fourteen.'

'Well, there are.'

'Oh Joe. You're kidding me. Pa said,' and she smiled and climbed the wall again, kneeling on the top this time.

'Aye, then he must be right.' Joe would concede this to the girl.

There were fourteen islands they sometimes called the Flannans, and sometimes the Seven Hunters: fourteen rocks and only two or three big enough to walk ashore and stake a claim to.

'There's the rest of the fleet,' Joe said, pointing to a flotilla of boats that had rounded the point of Rubha Arspaig.

Annabella laughed. 'That's not a fleet,' she said scornfully. 'That's just the fishermen. Shall we go and see what they've caught?'

'You'd best ask your Ma first.'

'If I do Arthur'll want to come and he's a nuisance.' Arthur was two years younger than Annabella. There was Robert and Louisa too, but they were older.

'Well, I'll not risk the wrath of your mother. So you'd best be asking her. Go on now.'

Annabella jumped off the wall and ran up the slight incline towards the house. She disappeared around the corner and Joe heard the scullery door slam. His attention was drawn back to the fishing boats and he counted them in: four, plus the one that had already moored against the pier. That made five. Five boats that had braved the dying storm to check the lobster pots and bring in the catch. Joe knew what it meant to be a fisherman. He knew the dangers and the hardships. He knew it was backbreaking work that got into your soul, and that the wife of a fisherman often didn't know if her man would come home to her or be claimed by the waters he harvested. His father had put to sea after the fish, though this was between bouts of trying his hand at being a factory man. But Joe knew he couldn't be a fisherman. He was a lighthouse keeper and that was enough. It was enough to watch the sea and wonder at its magnificence, fear its deepheld secrets. He didn't need to rob it of the life it held, not when it so often extracted the price of human sacrifice by way of return.

Joe heard the scullery door slam once more, but it wasn't Annabella that leant on the wall this time. It was Will Ross, one of the other Assistant Keepers. He'd broken his arm in

October and had been replaced at the lighthouse temporarily by the Occasional, Donald Macarthur, who was a local man.

'You're sitting on that wall again, Joe,' he said, as if in echo of little Annabella's words earlier. 'My old Ma would say you'll catch your death.' Will looked fierce, with his great dark beard and pipe stuck out of the corner of his mouth, but Joe knew he was a friendly soul who hadn't taken kindly to his enforced period of sick leave.

'I'm waiting on that wee girlie. She wanted to see the catch.' He wrinkled his nose. 'There's a storm coming.'

'Och, there's always a storm coming,' Will said, chewing on his unlit pipe.

Joe shivered, feeling the freezing December wind in the air. There had been no snow yet, but then they didn't always get snow. Sometimes it was just rain sheeting down in great icy blasts from the Atlantic.

'I wish I was with you this Christmas and not stuck here nursing my arm like a woman,' Will moaned.

Joe nodded, but didn't say anything.

Will went on: 'Could we no celebrate early this year? Tommie won't mind.' He meant Thomas Marshall, the man Joe would relieve at the lighthouse.

'I suppose so. Annie Macarthur down in the clachan must be feeling lonely, what with her Donald being away.'

'Aye. Or perhaps it's because you've got your eye on her?' Will fixed a fierce look on Joe.

'Och, I've no interest in an old married woman like her.'

'She's barely thirty years old.'

'Thirty-two.'

'Ah, you know that much then.'

'Away wi you.' Joe noticed Annabella returning and he laughed to himself before saying out loud so that she could hear: 'We could have a ceilidh.'

'A ceilidh?' Annabella's voice chirped up. She had come up behind them and now slipped her hand into Joe's. 'Can I come?'

'Of course. Everyone's invited.'

'And Mrs Macphail?'

Ina Macphail was a favourite. She occasionally gave the children of the lighthouse extra lessons. She often came up to Taigh Mòr to keep company with Mary Ducat and Annie Macarthur. They were sewing a quilt together. Ina's sister had gone to America and written and told her that the American women were much taken with sewing quilts. It seemed a wonderful idea. They would sew a lighthouse quilt. Mary's eldest daughter Louisa joined them from time to time, and Annabella and Arthur sat underneath and listened to the gossip, while the oldest Ducat boy, Robert, sorted out the material into different colours and shapes.

'And Mrs Macphail,' answered Will.

'Well. Are you ready for those fish, wee Annabella?' asked Joe.

'I am,' she replied.

'Then we'll be away.'

Joe jumped down from the wall and the little girl danced on the muddy road in front of her favourite keeper, while Will watched them from the gate.

He called: 'Bring back a bucket of herring. Wait,' and he jogged to the kitchen returning with a bucket in his good hand. 'There's nothing nicer than fresh herring for tea.'

Joe took the bucket from Will with a grimace. 'My God, I hate herring.'

'That's as maybe but Mrs Ducat has a liking for them and I may take a few down to Annie.'

'Oh you may, may you? I might have a thing or two to say about that,' and Joe gave his fellow keeper a knowing wink, which Will chose to ignore. Instead he addressed himself to Annabella.

'Make sure they're nice and plump.'

'I'll squeeze their bellies to make sure,' the little girl said, smiling broadly.

Joe took off down the road, the empty bucket clanking in time to his footsteps.

'We're going to see the fish, the fish. We're going to see the fish,' Annabella sang in a high voice. And she was still singing when they reached the small harbour and stepped out onto the pier.

*

SS *Archtor* slipped into the Leith dockyards late in the afternoon. Cal couldn't wait to step ashore. He'd had enough of shipboard life and needed to find a bar, a woman and a bed, in that order. His last hours in the small cabin he'd occupied during his transatlantic crossing had been fraught with indecision – what to pack in his small valise, which he would carry ashore by hand, and what to pack in his large trunk, which would be delivered to his boarding house, once he had established where he would stay. A change of clothes, his shaving kit, his notebook, and a bottle of Scotch would suffice for the next few days. He wrapped the whisky carefully in a pair of socks and then thought better of it. It would be safer if he drank it now. He could buy another bottle or two onshore. Why, he could buy a whole crate of Scotch if he so desired. He took another swig, felt the warmth of the liquid fire his throat and wondered why, when both his mother and father had been born here, he didn't feel more Scottish himself. He drank again.

God, but they make good booze, he thought and stoppered the bottle before stuffing it down between the socks. He snapped the bag shut and ran a hand through his hair before tapping his breast pocket to check that his list of lighthouses they'd passed en route from the Flannans was still there. The carefully folded piece of paper rustled as he touched it through the fabric of his suit. Yes, it was there; evidence that some grievous misdeed had taken place. Cal had duly noted each lighthouse the *Archtor* had passed since the missing light at the Flannans. Now it was time to go up on deck and greet Scotland.

The docks at Leith were lined with all kinds of vessels, the skyline broken by the masts of older wooden sailing ships, while interspersed between them were the funnels of steamers, both merchant and passenger craft of all sizes. The bustle of the docks surprised Cal. He'd expected a tiny backwater and instead he was greeted by a lively port. Nevertheless it was a damp grey place and he felt a little unsure of himself. He shivered and pulled the collar of his overcoat up, stuffing his hands into his pockets.

'I assume you are leaving us today?'

Cal turned and saw the Master of the ship approaching him. He was pulling his thick gloves on and had a scarf wrapped round his neck.

'Is it always this cold?' Cal asked, deflecting Holman's question with one of his own. Holman gave a sarcastic laugh and walked past Cal towards the gangplank.

'You'll get used to it.'

Picking up his valise, Cal ran after Holman, slipping as he trod the gangplank. Righting himself he twisted to avoid running slap bang into a docker, before reaching out to catch Holman's arm. The Master swung round momentarily to loosen Cal's grip, and then continued walking.

'Wait,' Cal called. 'Wait. Where are you going?'

Holman didn't reply.

'There have been certain irregularities.'

'What irregularities?' Holman boomed, coming to a standstill.

'Back there on the ship.' Cal pointed in the general direction of *Archtor*. He was out of breath and his valise suddenly felt very heavy. He shifted from leg to leg nervously, trying to work out why he felt so ill at ease. This wasn't like him. No, not like him at all. Perhaps it was the strangeness of the land, the cold weather, or more likely Cal thought, the people. His hand went automatically to his breast pocket. The list was still there.

'Back there on the ship?' Holman screwed his face up. Cal glanced around.

'Yes,' he finally ventured. 'Back on the ship. The light-house.'

'The lighthouse?'

'Yes, the lighthouse.' He frowned. Was Holman being deliberately stupid or was he covering for someone?

'The lighthouse. You call that an irregularity?'

'Yes, God damn it. The lighthouse. What are you going to do about it?'

'Why, nothing,' said Holman, and he turned away from Cal, walking now towards Commercial Street.

'Nothing?' Cal said, resuming his chase.

'You heard me.'

'You can't do nothing. I made a list.' A cart passed by. Its wheels ran straight through a large puddle, splashing Cal in the process. By the time he had shaken himself down Holman had all but disappeared.

Cal shouted as loud as he could: 'You can't do nothing.'

Holman gave him a dismissive wave of the hand as he continued walking.

'You bastard. You can't do nothing,' Cal muttered, whirling round to begin his walk towards the boarding house one of the crew had recommended to him earlier. It wasn't until he'd gone some fifty yards or so, mumbling to himself all the way, that he realised he had no idea how to get there. Spotting Macduff in the distance, he shouted at him to wait. By the time he'd caught up with the big seaman he was out of breath again.

'Where's the Captain going?' he gasped, holding onto Macduff tightly for fear of losing yet another member of *Archtor*'s crew.

Macduff frowned. Cal closed his eyes and took a deep breath before trying his question once more.

'Where is Captain Holman going right now?'

Macduff considered. Cal sighed and shook his head.

'How hard can it be? Where is he going? I need to talk to him.'

'Oh. He'll be going to the agents.'

'The agents.'

'Aye. The agents. He always reports to the agents after we dock.'

'And where can I find the agents?'

'Och now, they're in Edinburgh.' Macduff shook his head as if Edinburgh was a long, long way away.

'Edinburgh?'

'Aye. Away up the road yon.'

'Is it far?'

Macduff sucked air in between his teeth before answering: 'Aye. Far it is.'

'How far?'

'Ten minutes.'

'Ten minutes?'

'Aye. Edinburgh's a mile away up there yon,' and he pointed south-west where, if it had been lighter, Cal would have been able to spot Edinburgh Castle on the skyline.

Cal shook his head. This man was an idiot. Plain as day – an idiot. He tried a different tack.

'Will he report the missing light?'

'The light?'

'The lighthouse,' Cal said, exasperated.

Macduff frowned. 'He will.'

'He will? Are you sure?'

'Of course. It'll be the log.'

Cal sighed. At last he was getting somewhere.

'Can you show me where I can find the agents?'

'Henderson and Mackintosh?'

'If they are the agents then yes, them. Can you show me how to find their offices?'

'I can that.'

'Great. Let's go.' He gave Macduff a smile of encouragement.

'Och, but they'll no be open now,' the big man replied.

'But you said…' Cal screwed his face up. Patience, he reminded himself, was a virtue, though not one he was long on admittedly. Still, the list was safe. He reckoned he could wait another day for his 'story'.

'Oh never mind. Tomorrow will do. The boarding house. Where is it?'

'Aye, Betty's place. She'll give you a bed for the night right enough.' Macduff chuckled.

'Can you show me?'

'Aye.'

'Now?'

'I was on the way there myself.'

Cal slapped Macduff on the back.

'Lead on.'

THREE

❧

*A*nnabella's unbraided hair dropped its ringlets down to her waist. A white handkerchief was tied round her eyes and she shuffled blindly, one hand held out in front of her, the other gripping the tail, ready to pin it on the donkey. Mary Ducat held a finger to her lips and hushed the other children, her eyes widening in delight as Annabella attempted to find the donkey's rear end.

Joe, standing in the door, saw Annie Macarthur smile up at him. Life was difficult for her here in Lewis. She'd been born in Kent, and although she'd lived here for seven years there were still times when she fought to make herself understood. If they weren't talking to her in Gaelic their speech was blurred with a Scottish accent her southern English ear couldn't quite make out. Joe began to make his way over to her. He felt sorry for her. She tried hard to fit in and the locals had taken to her in a big way, but she was still ill at ease with Mary Ducat, who was a motherly sort, always fussing over the keepers and making far too many cakes so that often one of her children was sent down to Annie's with the extras for her children. Mary's competence made Annie feel inadequate and she'd once confided as much to Joe. It was true that he'd leapt to Mary Ducat's defence, but he felt privileged to be party to Annie's worries and wondered if she talked to her husband in the same way.

Annabella found the board with her outstretched hand and crawled her fingers across the surface for some clue as to where the tail might belong before bringing it forward and fixing it firmly with the tack to the paper. Then she grabbed the handkerchief with both hands and pulled it down, screaming in delight when she saw that the tail, although half way down the donkey's back, was the closest yet. Ina Macphail marked the board with a pencil before removing the tack and handing it to Mary.

Annabella clapped her hands.

'Your turn, your turn, Joe,' she cooed.

'Ah, I'm no good at this game,' he protested, smiling briefly at Annie, who blushed as he did so.

'Och, go on with you. Here, here's the tail. Mind the tack now,' and Mary handed him the paper tail. 'You're the last one.'

Annie made him bend over and carefully covered his eyes with the handkerchief, tying it in a knot at the back of his head. He put a hand up to feel the handkerchief covering his face. Blind I am, he thought. God, don't let the demons come now. He shoved his other hand in his pocket, feeling for the smooth stone he kept there. Yes, there it was. He was alright. His anxiety had passed.

'Can you see?' Annie asked.

'No.'

'Good. Then we'll turn you round,' and Annie's hands turned him and he followed.

'And round.' Once again. Annie grinned at Annabella and her little brother Arthur, sitting side-by-side on the floor next to their mother on the seat above.

'And round.' He staggered, dizzy, and put both arms out brushing Annie's face with the tips of his fingers. If this was my woman, he thought, but then dismissed it. He couldn't let himself feel anything for her beyond friendship. She was another's wife.

'Mind the tack now,' called Mary. Joe heard Annabella giggle.

'Am I going in the right direction?' he asked, bumping into Will, who leant on the mantelpiece smoking his pipe.

'I reckon as no,' Will said. There was a certain tone to his voice that was not lost on Joe.

'Aye, sorry,' he mumbled, but he wondered what exactly he was apologising for. His occasional flirtation with Annie was harmless enough. He had no call on her but neither did Will.

'That way, that way,' called Annabella, pointing. She clamped her hands over her mouth to stop the giggles from bursting out. Arthur kicked her and she kicked him back.

'Can we no have cake now, Mam?' the wee boy asked.

'Hush child. After we've decided the winner,' came his mother's reply.

Joe found the board and gripped the top. He felt the paper and tried to make out with his sensitive fingertips the tiny holes the tack had made. There was the last hole on the board, Annabella's. He moved to the left just slightly and pushed the tack into the yielding surface. He hoped he hadn't guessed wrong.

Annabella screamed with delight. 'I've won, I've won. I get the biggest piece of cake.' She jumped up and hugged Joe tight as he took the handkerchief off and stared at the board. His tail hung over the withers. Annabella had indeed won the biggest slice of Christmas cake. Arthur scowled and grumpily folded his arms.

'She always wins,' he moaned. 'I don't want any.'

'Och, away wi you,' Mary said. 'I've a special piece saved just for you.'

Sitting round the table, the children were silenced by cake as they each tried to cram as much into their mouths as possible. Crumbs flecked the tablecloth like bread tossed out for the birds. Arthur grinned at his mother with his mouth stuffed full. Mary sighed. She'd be sweeping up for days.

Joe scanned the room. They had all come. Here was Will, who wouldn't be parted from his pipe and who had eyes for Annie just as Joe had, even though he didn't like to admit it. Fortunately Donald, Annie's husband, was not asked to go out to the lighthouse all that often, otherwise there might have been questions asked as to why she spent so much time with the other keepers. Here too was Mary and her four children. They'd spent two days decorating the house for this Christmas ceilidh amidst arguments over who had made the most paper streamers. Over by the window sat the sometime schoolteacher Ina Macphail, her hands folded on her lap. The children loved her as if she was their own mother. Ina knew gentle Gaelic songs, which she sang in a bird-like voice, and when she spoke she sounded like the sea as it whispered on the sand on a hot summer's day. Sitting next to Ina was her husband, the man they called 'The Missionary', Thomas Macphail, a beached whale of a man who took up two chairs and had to be helped to stand up. He presided over the gathering as if father to them all.

The ceilidh had been a good idea. They had all come and would do so again when Tommie, the returning keeper, celebrated Christmas proper and then again for Principal Keeper Ducat after Christmas. Looking round the room, Joe felt a surge of emotion go out to everyone, but particularly to Annie, and even though this confused him he turned to look at her as she talked quietly to Mary. Annie was folding her napkin, her dark hair coiled neatly at the nape of her neck, her hazel eyes shining. She must have guessed that Joe was looking at her because she glanced up and caught his gaze, holding it for a moment with her own. Then her eyelashes fluttered atop her cheeks and she blushed and turned away.

She's read my mind, Joe thought. She knows everything. He closed his eyes. No. Pray that she doesn't. Please God let her not know the torment. In his mind the prayer rose to heaven, and when he opened his eyes Annie was making her way across the room to him.

'You haven't eaten much, Joe. Aren't you hungry?'

He shook his head. It was always like this in the week before he went 'off'. He couldn't eat, couldn't think, couldn't rest for fear of waking the demons that slumbered inside.

'Would you like another cup of tea?' she asked, and she placed her hand on his chest. He could feel his heart beating hard as it reverberated through her palm.

'No.'

'What then?' She smiled calmly.

You know what I want, he thought. You know somehow. I want you to take the demons away and lock them up so they can't reach me.

'Let's go for a walk,' he said. 'I need to clear my head.'

'I can't. They're watching. They'll wonder where we're going.' She made it sound so innocent but when she licked her lips the tip of her tongue lingered, so that Joe felt himself compelled to beg.

'Please come with me,' and even as he said it his eyes flicked guiltily over to Will. Annie paused for a moment.

'Wait,' she said.

Joe watched her go over to Mary and make an excuse about feeling too hot.

'Joseph here has offered to escort me outside for a moment.'

'Well, you mind the cold now, dearie,' Mary said, but her attention was on her children, especially Arthur who looked as if he was going to be sick. While Annie whispered to her own children to be good for Mary and Ina, Joe waited out in the hallway. He couldn't bear Will's inspection any longer. They'd have an argument about it later. Joe knew they would. He'd try and keep out of Will's way this evening – go

40

for a walk in the dark if he had to. He didn't want to argue this close to going 'off'.

Annie closed the parlour door behind her, shutting out the conversations and the fiddle music that had just started up. Joe listened for a moment. It wasn't Will, although he could play – not with his arm in a sling though. Besides, Will's old fiddle never sounded this sweet. No, this was probably the oldest Ducat son, Robert. He had delicate hands and found his way easily around the fiddle. It would be the Cremona – only allowed out of the cupboard on special occasions and too good really for fiddle music; after all the Cremona was a proper violin.

Joe opened the front door and stepped out. The daylight was fading fast and it was still only two – an early twilight. Annie slipped her arm through Joe's. The cold fresh air made them both gasp.

'Where will we go?' asked Annie. She stood on tiptoe and pulled the collar of Joe's jacket up around his neck. He did the same for her, only with her shawl, pulling the fold higher and tucking it under her chin.

'Wherever the road leads us,' Joe replied, feeling suddenly shy.

They walked the path to the gate and Joe opened it, listening to the creak, thinking he must oil the hinges, hearing it clang shut, watching Annie's booted feet on the rutted road beyond. The rain had let up briefly and a faltering sun was making haste to throw a last fragile cloak of golden rays over the westering sky and into the sea below. Beyond the farthest reaches of the islands the clouds gathered against the horizon and threatened more storms to come. Joe held tight to Annie's arm and led her past the end of the garden to where the road divided; one way to the black houses and the pier, the other to the closer shore.

'It's too wet for the beach, Joe,' Annie protested.

'No. We'll stay on the rocks. You can sit on my jacket,' and reaching the first of the boulders he made much show of removing his jacket and spreading it out for her to sit down. Annie stood there, hands on hips, shaking her head in amazement and when Joe realised that she had no intention of sitting down on the cold, damp, slippery rocks, jacket to sit on or no, he sat on it himself instead and frowned.

Annie laughed. 'You'll die of the cold, Joseph Moore. You'll surely die of the cold.'

'Sit down, woman, and stop your moaning,' and he reached up and grabbed her by the hand, pulling her down beside him.

'There now,' he said. 'Isn't it better than standing up?'

'You're mad, Joe. Do you know that? You're mad.'

'Aye, quite possibly.' She didn't know how close to the truth that could be.

'We've a nice warm house back there you know.'

'I've a nice warm woman right here beside me,' he replied but regretted it instantly and said quickly: 'I'm sorry. I meant… You are warm aren't you? Do you want to go in? I wouldn't want you to catch cold.'

'I'm fine. I like watching the sea.'

'Is that all you like doing?'

'Are you suggesting something else, Joseph Moore? Because if you are I'm here to tell you there will be none of that. I'm a married woman.'

'Would I suggest such a thing?'

'No, you would not,' she said quickly. 'I'm sorry.'

'There you are then.' He nodded emphatically.

After they'd sat in silence for a while Annie asked: 'What's the matter?' Joe considered. Did she sense something running deep inside him or was he imagining the closeness he felt to her? He decided to err on the side of caution.

'I'm worried about going 'off' that's all. It's always like this wi me. Isnae your Donald the same?'

'Not that I've noticed.'

Joe nodded. Perhaps he was imagining all of it: the demons, the dreams, the drownings, the anxieties, the welling up of emotion, and the pressure inside as if he was about to explode or go mad. He was about to ask Annie for her opinion of madness when he noticed that there were three figures standing thigh deep in the sea looking at him. At first he just felt a sense of disconnection, as if he'd left his body and was watching himself watching them. He glanced behind and then back to the sea, taking in Annie at the same time. It didn't seem as if she'd noticed anything unusual and yet the three men were still standing there. They were dressed in dark oilskins and had sou-westers pulled down over their faces so that he couldn't tell them apart, only he knew who they were alright.

Annie said, 'Joe? Joe, what's the matter? You've gone very pale. What's the matter?' But Joe didn't answer her. It was now that he felt a reconnection with his body and the shock at the sight of the figures standing in the sea hit him.

'Can you no see them?' he whispered.

'See who?' Annie asked and she frowned, following Joe's stare towards the sea. 'There's no one there.'

But Joe knew they were there. They were standing right there, watching him. Seaweed floated around their legs, and their skin, or at least what he could see of it, was bloated and deathly pale. Joe put his hands up to his eyes to shut out the hallucination, but it didn't go away. He knew they were still standing there. He knew they were his friends, but he also knew that there was something unremittingly evil about them.

Without warning Joe began to shout, running into the sea, waving his arms and throwing punches at the figures, but his fists melted through them and they faded away as he did so. When his anger and fear were spent he stood there alone, waves washing round his legs, tears running down his cheeks. All energy spent he turned round slowly to face Annie and saw the frightened look on her face. He'd lost her now. He never really had her but now he'd lost her. She would think he was mad for sure. He waded back towards her. She didn't say anything to him, but turned away and began to walk back to the house. Halfway across the beach she stopped. There was a man stumbling up the road towards them. This time it was a real man.

Exhausted, Joe mumbled: 'It's Archie.'

'Who?'

'Archie Lamont. From the *Hesperus*. Come to take me to the lighthouse.'

'Now?'

Joe shook his head. 'Should be tomorrow.' Staggering forward he tried to pull his trousers higher on his waist and neaten his appearance, forgetting that his trousers were wet, but aware suddenly that he was a representative of the NLB. He had to look his best, hallucination or no hallucination.

44

'My jacket, my jacket, woman,' he muttered angrily. Annie bent over, picked the jacket up and handed it to him.

'I don't know what's come over you, I really don't,' she said.

'Not now,' Joe replied.

'Laddie, is that you?' called Archie.

'Aye. It is. What can I be doing for you? It isn't until tomorrow that we're sailing, is it?'

Archie was breathing hard, his face red with the exertion of hurrying.

'We'll no be sailing tomorrow. There's another storm coming and we won't be able to land. We're on standby 'til the skipper says so.'

Joe didn't say anything. Archie glanced down at Joe's wet trousers but he didn't comment.

'You wouldn't think there was a storm out there at all, would you?' Annie piped up. 'It seems much calmer here of late.'

Archie smiled curiously.

Joe came to his senses. 'Ah, this is Mrs Macarthur. The Occasional's wife.'

Archie spat on his hand, wiped it on his trousers and offered it to Annie. She shook hands tentatively. Archie was a stout man with a craggy kind face and a twinkle in his eye.

'Mrs Macarthur. It's good to meet you. I know Donald o'course. Well now, this here's the calmness of Loch Roag. Whereas out there's the Atlantic Ocean. We've sailed from Oban overnight and the Minch was powerful stormy. Master Harvie won't be taking the tender out in it again until it dies down.'

'How long?' asked Joe, his hands in his pockets now, feeling the stone, noting its smoothness, counting on it to keep him calm. Last week's wait had been bad enough but to have it prolonged indefinitely, that was something else.

Archie shook his head.

'Och now, I wouldn't like to say. Two or three days perhaps. Maybe more. Could be here until Christmas.' He shook his head again and then, as if only just realising he'd interrupted something private, he wished them both well and turned on his heels.

'Christmas!' Joe muttered angrily, watching Archie go. 'I don't want to be here for Christmas.'

'Why ever not?' Annie turned her face up to him and he almost took it in his hands and kissed her forehead, but he stopped himself and started walking back towards Taigh Mòr instead.

'Because I don't and that's all there is to it.'

*

Cal didn't have very far to travel to the offices of shipping agents Henderson and Macintosh. Although they were described as being 'of Edinburgh' their address was actually still in Leith. The discrepancy was lost on Cal, who knew nothing of Edinburgh snobbery and the need for the right address to impress business associates.

He had spent the previous evening in the company of Macduff and his cronies at Betty's boarding house, finding it uncomfortable but cheap. They had drunk themselves stupid and caroused the night away with several pretty young women. When dawn broke Cal woke to find himself lying on the window seat in his room, his pants round his ankles, spit pooled in the palm of his hand, which he had tucked under his cheek like a baby. It took him all day to work off the hangover and it wasn't until late in the afternoon that he realised that if he indeed wanted a crack at a 'real' story he should chase up his lead and go to the shipping agents. He needed to see what the Master of SS *Archtor* had reported to them about the missing light. He knew he should telegraph his editor in Philadelphia and let him know he'd arrived safe and sound, but he also knew that such an action would prompt Culpepper to telegraph by return with a request for his first report. As he had written nothing so far, Cal was loath to tempt fate.

He changed his shirt, scraped his face red raw with his blunt cut-throat razor and spat on his shoes, buffing them to a shine with his dirty shirt. He couldn't find Macduff so he decided to go in search of Henderson and Mackintosh on his own. Outside Betty's he asked for directions to the nearest hansom cab stand, told the cabbie the name of the shipping agents and trusted that the man would know how to get there.

The lamplighter had started his rounds as Cal paid the cabbie and stepped up to the agents' front door. He rang the bell and waited patiently. A toothless old crone answered, opening the door just a fraction and squinting at him from over the top of a pair of half-moon glasses. She chewed on her gums as she looked Cal up and down.

'Messrs Henderson and Mackintosh?' Cal enquired.

She sucked her cheeks in before answering: 'You've found them. Come in. Come in.' She shuffled aside and waved Cal over the threshold. Inside it was dark and the air was redolent with the sweet smell of pipe tobacco.

'They're on the first floor,' she hissed into his ear. Cal wondered how she managed the daily flow of business that must pass through this office. As if she had guessed his thoughts she explained:

'Mr Mackintosh is away the now. He'll be back presently. If you'll be going up to the office would you ask the gentlemen if they want their tea?' She lisped her words, her cheeks sucking in and out as she spoke.

Cal nodded nervously and started up the stairs. Almost at once a thundering voice bellowed out: 'Mrs Macdougal? Where is that tea?'

The crone tut-tutted and shook her head before disappearing down the dark hall. On the first floor landing Cal pushed open the first door and was greeted by the upturned faces of two clerks.

'Close of business was half an hour ago,' one of them said. Then he glanced behind Cal and hurriedly down at his ledger. Cal whirled round, his hand already extended to shake that of the man who had come up behind him.

'Mr Mackintosh? Let me introduce myself. Callum Robinson.'

The man wore dark tweeds and had a pipe stuck in the corner of his mouth. He muttered: 'It's Henderson, and we're closed.' He took the pipe out of his mouth and stared intently into the bowl.

'A moment of your time, that's all I need,' Cal said.

Henderson pressed the tobacco in the pipe's bowl down with the middle finger of his right hand before answering.

'You don't look like a seafaring man.'

'No. I'm…'

'The American.' Henderson turned away and entered another room. Cal followed after him.

'Yes, but…'

'But nothing. We're closed to business until the morning.' Henderson reached into a box on his desk and proceeded to pack the bowl of his pipe with new tobacco, muttering as he did so: 'Where is that woman with the tea?'

'The Master of SS *Archtor* sent me,' Cal ventured.

'He did?'

'Yes. He…'

'He was here just yesterday.'

'Yes. He…'

'He said you are a troublemaker.' And with this Henderson placed his pipe carefully on his desk and looked at Cal hard. When Cal didn't offer anything by way of explanation Henderson picked his pipe up again, inspected the contents and then proceeded to light it by first extending a tallow into the fire and then puffing voluminous quantities of smoke out while offering the tallow to the bowl. Cal watched his actions with growing annoyance.

'Master Holman should have reported the missing light at the Flannans.'

Henderson nodded, still puffing out smoke.

'I have reason to believe there has been foul play,' Cal continued.

The agent glanced up, surprised. 'Foul play?'

'Yes. I need to know what, if anything, he said to you about it.'

'I can't divulge that.'

Cal considered, glancing around the room. It was poorly lit, no curtains, stacks of ledgers in the corner and arranged along shelves behind the desk.

'I write for the *Philadelphia Star*, but my passage here has been paid for by the Cosmopolitan Line Steamer Company.'

'Indeed. I am aware of the arrangements.'

'You understand then that it would be in your interest to comply with my request for assistance in this matter.'

Henderson puffed on his pipe once more. Cal shifted from foot to foot.

Eventually Henderson said: 'There was nothing to report.'

'God damn it, the light was out,' Cal said, exasperated. 'I mean to find out why.' Henderson didn't reply. He just stared hard at Cal.

'I have evidence,' Cal said, fumbling in his pocket. He pulled out the all-important list of lighthouses and thrust it at Henderson.

'There,' he said, stabbing the paper with a finger as the agent scanned it. 'The names of every lighthouse we passed after the Flannan Isles. All present and correct. I watched for them. I noted them down. I counted them.'

It was true. Cal had spent much of the last three days of his voyage scribbling down the names of the lighthouses they passed as he spotted them. There was the Butt of Lewis, Cape Wrath, Sule Skerry, the lights guarding the way through the Pentland Firth, the Pentland Skerries, Kinnaird Head, Rattray Head, Buchan Ness, Girdle Ness, Tod Head, Scurdie

Ness, Bell Rock, the Isle of May, Fidra and Inchkeith. Henderson nodded and handed the paper back to Cal.

'Most impressive. There are others you've missed. Some too far off course to see properly anyway. But in any case I cannae help you. Master Holman reported the Flannan light out, but there's nothing strange in that, I can assure you. You cannae always see a lighthouse when the weather is bad. You must have noticed that.'

'Missed some. Never,' Cal said, snatching the list back. 'The weather was fine. Clear as a bell.' He frowned. Was it some kind of conspiracy? He hadn't missed a single light. He scrutinised the list himself, as if those they'd passed without his notice would somehow miraculously appear on the paper.

Henderson sighed. 'I cannae say more.'

Cal looked at the ceiling for inspiration.

'You people are impossible,' he said after a while, 'absolutely impossible,' and with that he stamped out of the room, running straight into Mrs Macdougal on the landing. She had been coming up the stairs with the tea tray and now she threw it up in the air and held her apron tight.

'Lord, but you gave me a fright,' she shouted after Cal, as he ran down the rest of the stairs slamming the front door.

Outside, a steady rain beat on the granite pavements, the light from the newly lit streetlamps reflecting in each grey stone. Cal had left the agents' office in a temper, but now, as he marched down the street, he felt his anger leave him and despair take its place. Was there no one he could turn to? Would no one give him a straight answer? He stopped in his tracks and turned his face to the blackened sky. The rain ran through his hair into his eyes, making him blink it away.

Realising that the Scottish weather had already ruined his suit, he started to shiver. He was fed up and he needed a drink. He fumbled in his pocket for the flask but found it missing. Instead his hand touched paper. The damned list. Shaking now from the cold, he smoothed out the crumpled sodden paper. The ink had run and the names of the light-houses had all flowed into one another. There was no evidence now. No way to prove that all the lights had been lit save one.

'It's a conspiracy,' he shouted suddenly, crumpling the paper and tossing it into the water-filled gutter. 'A damned conspiracy.'

FOUR

❧

The soft light from the oil lamp in the parlour lent a golden glow to Annie's hair as she bent to whisper something to Will Ross. Joe fixed her with a stony glare she chose to ignore, or perhaps she just didn't notice how consumed he was with jealousy. Her eyes shone bright as she tilted her head towards the white-hot coals in the grate and Joe felt his heart pound hard in his chest. He slid his hand in his pocket and stroked the smooth stone he kept there for just this purpose. An hour had passed since the inhabitants of Taigh Mòr had finished their late Christmas Eve supper and Joe still hadn't managed to find a moment to talk to Annie alone. He wanted to apologise to her for acting so strangely with her the last time they'd been alone together, but so far he hadn't been able to find the right moment. Now here she was making up to Will and it was more than Joe thought himself able to bear.

He was about to make excuses and retire for the night when Annie stood up, smoothed down her skirt, patted her hair and said that it was high time she got her children home. She gathered the wee bairns, Malcolm and Annie-Christina, and kissed Mary Ducat lightly on the cheek before wishing the two keepers goodnight. Joe licked his lips and watched her leave. It was now or never.

It was as dark as pitch on the road; only a broad swathe of stars lit the way. Annie and the children had barely gone two hundred yards before Joe caught up with them. He touched her briefly on the arm and she started, placing a hand on her heart. Joe could hardly see her in the darkness, but he knew her warm smell and sensed her outline.

'Oh, it's you. You made me jump,' she said.

'I'm sorry. I didnae mean to.' Joe took up a place at her side but remained silent for a while as they walked. He wondered how to start the conversation.

'You must miss Donald,' he said at last.

'That's true,' she said. The children ran on ahead, fearless in the thick darkness. Soon they couldn't be seen at all.

Children of the night, thought Joe, and he looked up at the sky. All the children hereabouts seemed elemental, made of the earth, and the water, and the stars.

'It's been a while since I've seen the aurora,' he said suddenly, thinking of the northern lights and the way they danced across the sky.

Annie looked up.

'I saw it two weeks ago. Before the storm.'

'I wanted to say…' Joe didn't know what he wanted to say. Or at least he knew what he wanted to say but couldn't

54

bring himself to do so. And what he wanted to say was that when he wasn't wondering if he was going mad he was thinking about her – Annie.

'No,' she said simply, as if she'd read his mind. 'Don't say anything because if you do it will all be spoilt and I will have to do something and I can't do that. I won't do that. I shouldn't have led you on so. It was wrong of me.'

'You never led me on. I didnae want…'

Annie placed her hand on his lips to stop him from speaking. Those fingers felt soft despite the obvious rough patches. Soft and warm. A woman's fingers. Why didn't he have a woman like this one standing before him now?

'Come and get Donald's present to take to him,' she whispered, and she removed her hand and picked up her long skirts so that she could better run after the children.

Joe stared blindly at her and then closed his eyes for a moment. Her hand had also smelt faintly of bread flour. When he opened his eyes Annie had gone. What should he do? Run after her? Slip inside the croft under the cover of darkness? Force her to love him? Lie in Donald's place in the bed beside her? No, he couldn't do that. He turned back to Taigh Mòr. He couldn't do that to a friend. He couldn't betray Donald's trust and there was no way he was going to tempt fate. He would stay away from the Macarthur croft from now on. Annie could give Donald's present to the Master of the *Hesperus* on the morrow. Joe had received word that the steam tender would be sailing in two days' time for the lighthouse. He would put all thoughts of Annie to the back of his mind and concentrate on his work. Stuffing his hand in his pocket he felt the stone once more, smooth, as always, in his palm. Yes, that was better; his connection with reality right there in his pocket, keeping him safe.

*

Cal's money had almost run out. The budget the newspaper had allocated him wasn't enough to include the antics he had enjoyed most evenings and his editor wouldn't arrange for further funds unless he received a decent story. A decent story about the emigrants however, was something that presently eluded him. He'd been in Scotland too long already. Far too long. He should be halfway back to the States but the mystery, what he now considered to be *his* mystery, haunted him to such an extent that he could think of little else.

Trying to shake the lighthouse from his mind, Cal had enquired with Captain Holman as to when *Archtor* would be making passage back across the Atlantic, but the Captain had explained: 'It's Christmas and then there's Hogmanay. It's a serious thing Hogmanay. Not to be missed. Besides we're waiting on the shipping agents. Aren't scheduled to leave for a while.'

That was over a week ago. Cal sat at the window seat in his favourite bar on Rose Street and pondered over the perennial problem of words on paper. What to write about the miserable wretches he'd encountered so far: the dregs of humanity that wanted to leave their homeland and seek their fortune in foreign climes. It wasn't easy. He had stuck it out at Betty's boarding house for as long as he could but eventually the fleas got the better of him and he decided to take his belongings and find somewhere more to his taste

– somewhere closer to the city proper. He found instead a small inn that was both convenient for the dockyard sinkholes of iniquity and yet not too distant from the heady stone confection that was Edinburgh. Had he but known it he would have found far less salubrious venues to frequent in the capital. To Cal the old town was higgledy-piggledy quaintness, and the new all boulevards and arrogance, with little to offer in the way of female company. The truth of course was somewhat different. Women of the night could be found aplenty, whatever pleasure be desired, if you knew where to look.

Christmas Day had come and gone in a haze. Mostly he had stayed in bed, wondering what he was doing in this Godforsaken land. When he dreamed it was of lights flickering on and off and he would wake fevered and reach for his glass. As to work, he was sick of interviewing the ever-hopeful émigrés that inhabited Leith's backstreet taverns. Somewhat morosely, towards late afternoon, he had found the energy to dress and go out. For a while he hung around the dockside pestering anyone who would talk to him, but try as he might he couldn't fix his mind on a story that might interest his employer. It was the light, ever the light that dogged his thoughts. As the midnight chimes sounded in the distant church he made his way back to his lodgings.

Cal had come to Scotland to find the kind of emigrants his own family were descended from, and to tell a stirring tale of courage as the hopeful travellers faced the journey of a lifetime across the deep dark Atlantic, but the poor souls who crowded the dockside boarding houses were all too sad to speak of anything save how much better the new land was going be for them. Cal knew from the experience of his own family that once these people arrived in America they would become more Scottish than ever they had felt themselves to be in their homeland. They would be bound together as a community of wayfarers adrift from their cultural moorings. Cal's own father had been so proud when his son told him he was returning to the old country. Yet the only thing Cal felt he had in common with the people he'd interviewed in the Leith docks was 'a wee dram'.

Even so, he had swiftly become known in the offices of the many shipping agents, and with their help had managed to track down a few brighter prospects but he found them a sullen bunch, with little money between them and few possessions. America beckoned brightly because, so they said, the old country no longer wanted them. They were displaced persons – the last of the clearances: fragile children wearing little more than rags and bearing the weight of their parents' pride, newly weds whose belongings included presents for use on the journey – a bottle of whisky to ward off the sickness, a fruit cake baked black and hard, for keeping. There were stories here among these people, but none that Cal wanted to tell. They were happy to make the acquaintance of someone they thought was a real American gentleman, and when they offered what thoughts they had on the matter of emigration Cal would smile and tell them that the United States of America was indeed the promised land.

Thus Boxing Day dawned for Cal in a haze of inebriation. Sitting quietly now in his room, the curtains open, he gazed out at the slowly awakening streets. Holman had mentioned Hogmanay and Cal knew from his own family that this was a celebration not to be missed. He would look forward to the possibilities this festival would afford him and then try for a passage home.

But what of that light? Could he let that go without finding out what had happened? And he was certain that something had happened. Whatever *it* was, *it* had already happened. He was sure of it. Something must have happened. Somehow he knew he'd been but a stone's throw away from the scene of some horrible event. He didn't know how but he just knew it. What's more, it could be the scoop of a lifetime. Perhaps this was the story he was meant to be telling. Not a story about poverty stricken emigrants but a real story – a mystery.

But where exactly were the Flannans and how would he get there? Hadn't Holman said it was off the west coast of the Outer Hebrides? Could he get a passage on a ship? Or was it possible to travel by train? Yes, that was it. Train as far west as he could. That would be the best option. God damn it, the whole of Scotland must know where the blessed Flannan Isles are. How hard could it be?

He fell asleep with his arms resting on the window ledge, his head against the glass. When he woke the slate rooftops glistened from the damp of a light rain and he had a crick in his neck. A mess of papers greeted him from the floor; his list – the one that the rain had pulped. Between waking and sleeping, and worrying about stories, he'd been scribbling down those names he could remember. Lighthouses that had never existed, would never exist, noted down in a barely legible scrawl. A thought crossed his mind – he would find the Flannan light if it was the last thing he did. Damn

Culpepper to hell and back. He would gather up his belongings and go down to the railway station this minute. He would set out on a trip to the Outer Hebrides. He didn't know how exactly he was going to do this, but he knew enough to begin by travelling west, towards the islands he'd passed on his voyage here. There was no point in trying for a passage by sea. It would be too long and too confusing. No, it would be better to travel by rail. Safer. Warmer. More civilised. With shaking hands he gathered his papers together, took his valise and stuffed as much as he could into it. He'd never been a great one for breakfast. A nip from his almost empty flask fortified him before he abandoned his other belongings and took off for Waverley Station.

FIVE

∞

WEDNESDAY, 26TH DECEMBER

The islands ranged into view, black against a grey sky, the turmoil of the Atlantic pitching the lighthouse tender *Hesperus* this way and that. The sea boiled green in its depths and broke across the smaller islands, no more than rocks littering the approach to Eilean Mor. As the wind shifted nor'east the rain sheeted against the deck on which Joe stood, holding tight to the railing and scanning the shoreline for the lighthouse flag. Down in the engine room the whining pistons strained in their cylinders as the tender lifted momentarily on the crest of a wave, the spinning propeller briefly exposed to the elements. The engineer shovelled more coal into the yawning mouth of the firebox and wiped his brow. The ship's horn sounded bleakly: once, twice, three times.

Still watching the shore, Joe shouted over the booming sea and stuttering engine: 'The flag's no there. They haven't seen us. Fire the rocket, will you?'

His voice was lost in the tumult but the Master had anticipated the futility of the horn. The sound of the rocket rent the air, the flash brightly visible, even in this hostile environment. The ship waited for the reply. The crew narrowed their eyes and focused on the lighthouse, now glowing with an eerie white resonance in the morning's cold light. No reply came. No flag was run up on the mast. No man waved to them from the shore.

'We cannae make the west landing. The weather's too bad. They won't be able to see us.' Joe turned to Archie, standing beside him.

'I wish I was in front of a nice fire now.' He knew it was madness. When he was at Taigh Mòr he wanted to be at the lighthouse. When he was at the lighthouse he wanted to be at Taigh Mòr. When he was on the relief tender he just wanted to be on dry land – any land in fact. And he was already missing Annie, though he hadn't allowed himself to touch her beyond taking her arm to guide her down the road, and even that made him feel guilty.

Archie clapped a hand on Joe's shoulder.

'The time will fly by, laddie. And anyway the weather's breaking over yonder,' and he pointed out into the western sky where the clouds were lighter. 'It's a pretty wee island when the sun's out. Aye, I wish I were coming with you.'

The two men waited side-by-side as the *Hesperus* tried to tie up at the east landing. Three times the tender approached only to be driven away by the force of the waves.

In desperation the Master, James Harvie, had the rowboat lowered into the sea and Joe, Archie and William Macormick, the Second Mate, known to all as 'Mac', rowed the short distance to the landing stage. Once there Mac flung a loop around the capstan making sure to keep the tiny boat a good distance from land so as not to be crushed against the rocks. Joe judged the rise and fall of the boat and jumped nimbly across to the landing stage. He nodded briefly to Archie and Mac and made off up the steep stairs cut into the cliff-face, leaving the two men to wait for him to return with Tommie.

The lighthouse tower rose high above the island, the house nestling against the base. Joe ran against the wind to the outer door and found it closed tight. He lifted the latch and pushed the door shouting 'hello' as he entered. Just inside the outer door, the kitchen door stood open. Again, he shouted 'hello,' this time adding, 'It's me, Joseph Moore.'

The kitchen was empty and the air smelt cold and damp. The fire was out in the grate, the ashes thin and white like burnt bones. The clock had stopped at nine. Dishes had been washed and stacked on the wooden draining board. Beside the deal table, a chair had been overturned.

The silence inside the house was frightening, made more so by the rain lashing ferociously against the windowpane. Joe felt as if his world had suddenly dropped away from him. He'd never expected demons to be so silent. Somehow he expected a noise; something more violent and angry than this. He shook his head. He was being stupid. They were simply ill, that was all. They'd taken to their beds. Coming to his senses, he ran into each bedroom in turn, expecting to find the keepers sick in their berths, but all the three beds were empty. Frantic now, he shouted up the well of the tower and listened to his own voice as it echoed through the empty space, the spiral brass banister winding his gaze to the top.

No one answered. They had to be here. They had to be.

Despairingly, Joe ran outside. He couldn't think straight. They must be here. The wind drove the rain into his face and gusted across the rocky land towards the derelict black house and remains of the chapel. Should he search the island? Should he try and find them? No. He couldn't leave Archie and Mac for much longer without telling them what he'd found – and he'd found nothing; not a single living soul remained on the biggest of the Flannan Isles save himself. When he thought about it there was just nowhere to hide on this rocky island.

He ran back to the landing stage trying to persuade himself that the men couldn't just have disappeared. There must be an explanation for it – a logical explanation. They must have been swept out to sea somehow, but even as he thought this he struggled to push away the fear that his nightmare had come true. He staggered down the steps, the wind whipping his words away as he shouted to the two men waiting below that the keepers had disappeared.

'There's no one there. They've gone.' His eyes filled with foam-flecked tears.

'Say it again laddie, slower,' shouted Archie, his voice raised against the roar of the surf.

'They aren't there. They aren't anywhere. I cannae find them.' Joe sobbed.

Archie weighed the information up.

'You'd best go back up and double check. Take Mac here wi you.' He gave Joe a nod. Mac set off up the steps with Joe following reluctantly behind.

Back in the lighthouse Joe climbed the tower to the gallery. The lamp was clean and the oil fountain full. So whatever had happened must have taken place during daylight hours because otherwise the oil would have been used and the lamp have burnt out. From up here Joe could see the entire island spread out below him and *Hesperus* bobbing in the swollen sea. At that moment he couldn't imagine a more desolate place on God's earth than this island, fifteen miles from the nearest land, in the deep dark Atlantic Ocean.

'Is everything alright up there?' shouted Mac from below.

'Aye. I'm coming down now.' Joe descended the stairs into the kitchen and found Mac studying the slate.

'The last entry was on the fifteenth. They hadnae written it up in the logbook yet. Look.' Joe peered over Mac's shoulder at the chalk marks on the slate. Barometer, wind direction and thermometer readings all neatly scored. The fifteenth. That was eleven days ago.

'When was the last entry?'

'The thirteenth.' Mac turned the logbook's pages.

'Do you think the light's been out since then?'

'Depends what happened.'

'What should we do? I don't want to stay here alone.' Joe had never felt this scared before, even at sea in the worst of storms when he believed that monsters from the deep would snatch him from the deck and ring the last breath from his body. Despite the nightmare people he imagined inhabiting a living death on the seabed, he could understand the sea if he really had to. This on the other hand was a dreadful mystery. Something had taken the three keepers and whatever it was could take him too.

'I saw them,' Joe muttered.

'What?'

'I saw them dead.'

'Where?' Joe didn't answer. Mac took him by the shoulders and shook him. 'Was it here? At the lighthouse? Down the rocks? In the sea? Where, laddie, where?'

'Not here. No. It was a dream.'

'A dream?'

'Aye. I'm sorry. They're no on the island.'

Mac pursed his lips, thinking hard.

'We've got to get back to the *Hesperus* and tell the Master. He'll know what to do. Come on, laddie, let's get back to the ship.'

The two men locked the kitchen door behind them and set off towards the east landing stage.

'What about the west stage? Shouldn't we check there?' asked Joe, his voice barely audible above the roar of the wind and ocean.

'Later,' Macormick shouted back.

Joe practically slithered down the steps to the waiting boat below. He jumped in beside Archie without saying anything. Instead he looked back up at the steps, trying to work out what had happened here, still not sure that the men were really missing.

'What's happened?' Archie wanted to know.

Mac shook his head. 'Row. We can't talk here.' He took the other oar and Joe let slip the rope, the tiny boat cast momentarily adrift in the Atlantic swell, until the combined efforts of the men pulling on the oars kicked in and the craft surged forward. All Joe could think about as he rowed was the emptiness he'd found in the lighthouse. The stark emptiness. No man alive, he thought. No man alive and the dream's come true. That was what the fifteenth had meant to him – it was the night of his last terrible dream. The night he'd thought they'd all drowned and he with them. It was the night he first saw the three men – the forerunners.

On board the tender Joe relayed what they'd seen at the lighthouse to the Captain, the words catching in his throat, his hands shaking. James Harvie took it all in impassively.

When Joe had finished, Harvie lowered his voice and said: 'We need to get back to Lewis and wire the news to the Board. You have to man the light. You say it's not been lit since the fifteenth?' Joe shook his head fearfully, knowing what Harvie would ask of him.

'We can't leave it a night longer.' Harvie turned to the buoymaster, Alan Macdonald.

'Will you go ashore with Joe here until I can get you relief?'

'Aye. I'll keep him company.'

'Take Archie Lamont and Archie Campbell with you. You four are in this together now. Scour the island for signs of those men. Find out what happened. I'll be back as soon as I can. And Macdonald…' Harvie glanced up at the big red-haired man standing in front of him. 'Have the lad write the report. Give him something to think about.'

'Aye, sir, I will.'

Harvie turned back to Joe.

'Well, you're the keeper now. Macdonald, Lamont and Campbell will go with you but remember they aren't lighthouse men anymore than I am. So it's up to you to keep that lamp lit. I'm depending on you now. The Northern Lighthouse Board is depending on you. Are you up to it?'

Joe didn't want to set foot on Eilean Mor again but he said: 'Yes, sir. I'll do my best,' feeling as if ice ran through his veins and not blood. He'd have to brave it out. He'd have three others with him. He'd get through it somehow.

Joseph Moore, Alan Macdonald, Archie Lamont and Archie Campbell were set ashore on the afternoon of 26th December 1900. They took the regular supplies with them and winched the rowboat onto the derrick above the thundering sea. The *Hesperus* steamed towards Taigh Mòr, the shore station at Braescleit, so that Captain Harvie could wire the Northern Lighthouse Board from the telegraph office in Calanais and await further instructions.

*

It was late in the evening when the *Hesperus* tied up at Braescleit pier. The tide had turned and shoals of tiny fish were swimming upstream, silver bellies glistening beneath the surface of the loch. Out in the channel, where the sea-loch deepened, the current showed strong in the rippling waves. Water lapped the steamer's hull and the now sandy, now stony, shoreline as the engine died, and smoke from the stack dissipated in the light offshore breeze. The men on the *Hesperus* talked in hushed tones, their voices a melodic confluence through the steel sides of the ship. Lights showed in every porthole, and in every window of the bridge, throwing the pier into stark relief against the backdrop of the sea.

Eight-year-old Annabella Ducat, wrapped in her warmest coat and wearing thick woollen gloves and scarf, sat on the wall and waited patiently for the lighthouse keeper Thomas Marshall to walk ashore. Her toes were cold but she wasn't bothered.

Half an hour passed before Captain James Harvie gave Second Mate William Macormick and Seaman Ian Finch the nod and they disembarked, leaving their warm below-deck cocoon for the chill of the December evening. Together the three men set off on their two-mile walk to the telegraph office that Duncan Macrae kept at Calanais Farm. They passed houses shrouded in darkness and sighted Taigh Mòr built beyond the rise. They paced at speed, each man keeping his thoughts to himself, the night unfurling before them as they walked.

To Annabella they seemed like ghosts at first, parting the darkness with their blurred black shapes, but as she watched them the ghosts became real men. They walked in silence, their footsteps beating out the sound of each man's pounding heart. When they were close enough that she could smell their sea-tinged oilskins and thick tobacco odour Annabella jumped down from the wall. Which was Tommie? She liked him. He made her laugh and in many ways he was like Joe. He had no wife, although both his father and sister lived close by, and when he was off duty Tommie lived at Taigh Mòr with the Ducats. And just as Joe let Mary mother him, so did Tommie.

The men came closer, their faces sharpening, taking on features. Annabella was confused. None of these men were

Tommie. None. But she knew they were from the steamer. She'd seen them before. Harvie, Mac and Finch passed the little girl with barely a glance in her direction, and she watched them intently as they walked straight past Taigh Mòr and on up the road towards Calanais.

'Where's Tommie?' she called after them and Finch, still walking, still keeping step with the other two men, turned to look back at her, his face showing grey in the light from the windows of Taigh Mòr.

'Is he no with you?' she asked, but Finch turned away and kept on going.

Annabella frowned and started towards the pier, meaning to go down to the *Hesperus*, but something made her change her mind and instead she followed the men, trying to keep up with them as best she could.

'Wait,' she cried. But they didn't answer. They didn't pause. They were walking too fast. They weren't going to stop and let a wee girl catch up with them. Annabella soon got out of breath. She staggered on, but the road was slow going into Calanais and badly rutted. The men became ghost shapes again. The darkness took them back as surely as it had given them birth. She knew where they were headed. If it wasn't to the bothan where the men gathered in the evening to swap yarns, then it would be the telegraph office. She would check there first. The bothan was further away and her mother had told her never to go there.

In the tiny office Harvie took his coat off and hung it on a peg on the back of the door, so that he would feel the coat's benefit when he left. Duncan Macrae had been roused from his fireside to tap out the message that Harvie now dictated.

The men's breath soon misted the windowpane. Annabella, pressing her nose to the glass, could just make out Mac and Finch standing nervously against the wall. Harvie loomed over the man sitting at the desk. The condensation on the window turned everyone into white ghosts. She could hear the boom of Captain Harvie's deep voice but the tap-tapping of Macrae as he sounded the message prevented her from hearing Harvie's actual words. All at once the door opened and a shock of light illuminated the pathway. The three men stepped out into the cold. Annabella lifted her face to meet that of the Captain and nervously asked when Tommie was coming home.

'Ah, now there's a thing,' Harvie replied. 'Should you no be home in bed by now? Your mother will be wondering where you are.' He sounded gruff. He'd spent his life at sea. His wife was the ship he captained, and his family the sailors who followed his command.

The other two men mumbled in agreement, then fell into silence. Annabella looked from face to face but couldn't make out their thoughts.

Eventually Harvie said: 'Come on, wee lass. Let's get you home.'

'Will Tommie be there by now?' she asked. The men glanced at each other. Something had happened. Why didn't they tell her?

'No. He will not,' Macormick ventured, only to be shushed immediately by Harvie. Annabella sensed the tension, and caught the nervousness in each man, but she didn't understand what passed between them, what secret they kept.

'If Tommie's no come home, has someone else come back instead? Pa maybe?'

'Put your best foot forward, Miss Ducat, or your mother will have my hide,' announced Harvie, ignoring her question. Annabella slipped unhappily into step. The darkness sank away from them now, as if they walked in a bubble of light when really it was only the company of men. The message duly delivered by telegraph to the George Street headquarters of the NLB, it would be down to Harvie to tell the womenfolk about the disaster.

Mary Ducat stood on the threshold awaiting the return of Thomas Marshall. She'd noticed the arrival of the *Hesperus* from an upstairs window. When the men walked up the path with Annabella between them, Mary ran outside, took the girl by the hand, and gave Harvie a look that said, 'Don't tell me. Don't tell me in front of the children.'

'Get you away to the kitchen,' she said to Annabella. 'Make sure and help Louisa lay the table.' A keeper's home-coming always included a welcoming feast.

Annabella ran inside and the kitchen door slammed shut. Moments later she opened it slightly and peeped through.

'What are you doing?' asked her sister, as she closed the oven door.

'Ssh,' Annabella silenced her. 'They've come to tell Ma.'

'What have they come to tell her?' Louisa wiped her hands on her apron and came to the door.

'How do I know if you don't hush your mouth?'

The sisters peeped through the opening and saw the men standing in the hall, their caps in hand, their eyes downcast.

Louisa asked: 'Is Tommie no home yet?'

'They haven't told her,' whispered Annabella.

'Told her what?'

'The secret about Tommie.'

The blood left Louisa's face.

'What?' Annabella pressed. 'Tell me. What are they saying?'

'I don't know,' replied Louisa. 'But it must be something bad. Where's Robbie and Arthur?'

'I don't know.'

'I'll go. You stay here.'

Annabella pouted. Her sister was sixteen, a woman now. Annabella felt left out. Louisa slipped out of the kitchen and up the hall, her skirts rustling, which in turn alerted her mother. Mary Ducat turned ashen-faced to her eldest daughter. Annabella caught sight of her mother's wide eyes filled with tears.

'Oh God,' cried Mary and she buried her head in Louisa's arms. 'He's gone', she blubbed. 'He's gone Louisa. Gone.'

Annabella approached cautiously, barely able to breathe, not knowing what her mother's words meant. Who had gone? Tommie? Pa?

Finch bit his lip and Harvie eyed the hall mirror as if looking for an answer beyond the surface. Mac smiled gently at Annabella and shook his head. She looked from man to man, from woman to woman and no one said a word to her. Upstairs she could hear her brothers, Robbie and Arthur, banging some game out on the floorboards. Were they as innocent as she?

Eventually Harvie came to his senses.

'We'd best be off, Mrs Ducat. We've got to call on Mrs Macarthur too. I'll keep you informed. Rest assured of that.' He touched Mary's arm briefly, pain showing now in his features as he turned from her and motioned the others to leave the Ducats be.

In the cold hall, the door still open to the night, mother and oldest daughter sobbed, their arms wrapped around each other for comfort. The world seemed suddenly reduced to the small space occupied by these two women. Wee Annabella sat on the stairs and wished someone would tell her when Tommie was coming home and what could possibly have happened to her father to make her mother weep so.

*

The boy had strict instructions: take the telegram to the Northern Lighthouse Board at 84 George Street, Edinburgh and hand it personally to William Murdoch Esquire, Secretary. The trouble was there was no answer at the George Street office and now he had to pedal all the way across the New Town to Murdoch's house. At least the rain had stopped. The pavements shone newly washed in the gaslight. The boy gave one last look up at the impressive façade, thrust the telegram back into his pocket, and picked his bicycle up from the pavement. Ten minutes later, after he'd terrified half a dozen cabmen and their horses with his furious pedalling, the boy threw the bicycle into the bushes at the corner of the big house and rang the doorbell. He could hear the bell jangle inside all the way downstairs to the servants' quarters.

Snoozing in his study, the fire's red glow the only light, William Murdoch was jolted awake by the front door bell. Replete with the leftovers of the post-Christmas feast he closed his eyes, knowing full well that his maid Katie would answer it. He wasn't expecting any callers and without an invitation she would send them away. He was just beginning to drop off again when he heard Katie's gentle knock.

'Hm,' Murdoch mumbled. The door opened and light from the hallway suddenly flooded the room.

'Excuse me, sir, but there's a telegram come for you.' Katie held the piece of paper in her outstretched hand. 'Shall I send the boy away?'

'Yes.' Then he thought again. 'No, wait. It may need a reply. Who's it from?'

'A Captain Harvie, sir. Come for you at the office but you weren't there.'

Murdoch struggled to sit upright, fumbling with his wire-framed reading glasses, which had slipped down his nose onto his chest.

'Yes. Well. Let's see what this Captain Harvie's got to say for himself.' He took the telegram from Katie and squinted through his lenses at it.

'Blast! What does it say?' He shook the telegram and stood up, but it was no good. It was still too dark to read. He walked out into the hall, brandishing the telegram in front of him. The boy stood in the open doorway, cap in hand. Katie had told him to wait but he couldn't stand still. His legs were cold. Murdoch held the telegram under the lamp, but the boy's presence annoyed him.

'Come in, come in. Close that blasted door. Do you live in a barn?'

The boy stepped inside and closed the door. His boots were wet through and he made a puddle on the chequered floortiles. Murdoch scanned the telegram's contents. He took his time – read it twice – closed his eyes. Finally he sighed deeply.

'Wait there while I make a note.' Murdoch folded the telegram carefully and placed it in his breast pocket.

'Terrible,' he said quietly to himself. 'Terrible.'

In his study, the desktop lamp now lit, the fire dying in the grate for want of coal, William Murdoch, Secretary to the Northern Lighthouse Board Commissioners, penned a note by way of return. He would send his best man out to investigate. With any luck Superintendent Robert Muirhead could be in Lewis in two, maybe three days. There would have to be a full report. Replacement keepers had to be found. Yes, Robert Muirhead was the best man for the job. Signing the note with a flourish Murdoch handed it to the boy, together with a coin from his pocket.

'And there's a little something for yourself. Merry Christmas.'

The boy looked at Murdoch in astonishment for there in his palm lay a shiny sixpence.

26th December 1900

Telegram from Master, Lighthouse Tender 'Hesperus', reporting the accident at the Flannan Isles Lighthouse

A dreadful accident has happened at Flannans. The three Keepers, Ducat, Marshall and the Occasional have disappeared from the Island. On our arrival there this afternoon no sign of life was to be seen on the Island. Fired rocket but, as no response was made, managed to land Moore, who went up to the Station but found no Keepers there. The clocks were stopped and other signs indicated that the accident must have happened about a week ago. Poor fellows they must have been blown over the cliffs or drowned trying to secure a crane or something like that. Night coming on, we could not wait to make further investigation but will go off again tomorrow morning to try and learn something as to their fate. I have left Moore, Macdonald, Buoymaster and two Seamen on the island to keep the light burning until you make other arrangements. Will not return to Oban until I hear from you. I have repeated this wire to Muirhead in case you are not home. I will remain at the telegraph office tonight until it closes, if you wish to write to me.

SIX

❧

It was late in the evening and the Glasgow steamer *Clansman*, operated by Macbrayne's ferry company, lay at anchor in the harbour at Rhue. She was one of two steamers that plied their trade between the great city of Glasgow and the small town of Stornoway on the Isle of Lewis. The voyage took them first to Oban on the west coast, then through the Sound of Mull and round Ardnamurchan Point towards the small community at Arisaig on the west coast of Scotland. Here the steamers would offload passengers and cargo, as at Oban, before continuing across the Minch to Stornoway. Ships calling here didn't actually make it as far as Arisaig at all, but instead weighed anchor on the leeward approach to the township, at Rhue.

Cal had taken the steamer from Glasgow on the advice of the stationmaster at Edinburgh Waverley railway station.

This man had gone to some length to explain that by far the quickest and easiest way to the Outer Hebrides was by sea. The information had upset Cal a great deal because he'd hoped that he would only have to make a short ferry crossing to the Isle of Lewis. To discover that he would have to sail all the way from Glasgow seemed too much like the voyage he had made across the Atlantic – long and nauseating.

The stationmaster had said: 'Aye well, you can take the train to Oban if you've a mind. And I cannae say exactly that it would be a bad idea...' Here the stationmaster removed his cap and scratched his head. He had red tufted hair. Very deliberately he smoothed the brim of his hat before putting it carefully back on.

'But I'd go by steamer if I was you,' and here he pursed his lips and then sucked his cheeks in as if chewing something sour that he couldn't decide if he wanted to swallow or not.

Cal frowned. Didn't this man want his business? What was so wrong with the train that he wouldn't sell him a ticket? Why was everyone in this infernal country so difficult to deal with?

'Can you sell me a damned ticket or not?' Cal asked, but the stationmaster had already given his clerk in the ticket office the nod, as if to say 'we've a right one here', and nothing Cal said from that point on could persuade either official to sell Cal a ticket beyond Glasgow.

'You can catch a perfectly fine ferry out to Stornoway with only the shortest of stopovers in one or two wee towns along the way.' The stationmaster patted Cal on the shoulder. 'You look like a man who needs to relax a wee bit. Aye, the steamer is the perfect way to reach the isles. You'll no be sorry.'

Thus informed, Cal found himself travelling by train to Glasgow, where despite trying to buy an onward ticket north towards Fort William on the new West Highland line, he'd been thwarted yet again by a well-meaning porter who helped him into a cab and told the driver to take him to the docks before Cal had a chance to say otherwise. It all seemed very odd.

Cal could see little of Rhue against the darkness of the night sky, but it appeared to be nothing more than an old pier, a storehouse of sorts, a hand-operated crane, and a jumble of stone houses. Smaller boats were moored closer to shore, some drawn up onto the rocks. As far as ports went it didn't look like that busy a place, but there was a brisk trade in shellfish to London and ships large and small called here constantly. This much was evident from the boxes and barrels stacked dockside, awaiting both onward passage across the Minch, and portage inland.

A line of dark figures was winding its way along the road, each person bent nearly double with the load on their backs. Cal had seen the cargo stacked on board ship at Glasgow and then again at Oban. It was mostly cereal and salt, sugar and biscuits in wooden barrels, and packages of soap and candles. These were staple products for the hard-pressed Highlanders; things that made life a little easier for them. To Cal though it seemed as if the people hereabouts were desperate folk living on the most basic of foods, scratching a living from a soil-deprived landscape of rock and water. He shuddered. What a hellhole. A dark, cold, wet hellhole with nothing to redeem it.

A little girl squeezed between his legs. She was running away from her brother as he chased her, weaving through the other passengers all similarly transfixed by the sight of land, however black it appeared in the distance.

'Hey you,' Cal shouted at the girl, 'mind your manners.' He shook his trouser leg as if ridding himself of any dirt she might have left in her wake.

The girl turned briefly and stuck her tongue out. She shouted something Cal couldn't understand and an old woman holding the rail next to him cracked a gap-toothed smile and winked.

'It's the Gaelic she's speaking. You'll no understand her I'll warrant.'

Cal shrugged. God, how he hated these people. He stared at a rag-taggle group approaching *Clansman* in a large rowboat. Someone in the stern held a smoky oil lamp aloft. The man at the oars was struggling against the swell, making poor headway. A woman in the bows wedged a child under one arm, hitched up her skirt with her free hand and attempted to stand up. The wee bairn stared impassively at the glistening waves as his mother began to shout obscenities at the oarsman.

'They call it *An bata dearg* – the red barge.' The old woman nodded wisely. She went on: 'Tinkers they are.' She spat out into pitch-dark night.

'Not a person aboard will welcome the likes o' them.'

'Really?' Cal couldn't work out the difference between the ragged-clothed 'tinkers' and the old woman standing next to him.

'Och, but it a grand sight is Rhue. Not that you'd want to go ashore here the now. Smallpox I've heard.'

Cal scowled. The old woman took his grimace as a sign to continue her story.

'I know of a family struck down wi the smallpox. From a Russian they got it.'

'A Russian?' Cal enquired, his curiosity aroused.

'Aye, a Russian. Oh it's not so strange. There's many a foreign ship calls in here. They buy the herring you see. They like a wee fishy or two, those Russians.'

'And the smallpox?' Cal could feel the disease creeping up on him even as he spoke its name. He reached into his pocket and fished out his hip flask. It was empty. A full bottle of whisky lay in his hand luggage, and he could take leave of this old woman and fill his flask, but the story of the smallpox-bearing Russian nagged at him and he felt compelled to listen; ever the journalist.

'Well now, I heard that the family who caught it had to be isolated and this caused great distress to the others that weren't ill. They had to rest up in their neighbour's house and that caused the overcrowding. Of course this was just asking for trouble.'

'It was?'

'Aye, nothing smallpox likes more than overcrowding.' The old woman nodded wisely. She knew she had a captive audience in this strange man.

'Well now,' she continued, 'the smallpox took away two daughters, a son, a baby and the *cailleach*.'

'The *cailleach*?'

'An old lady. Aye, an old lady just like me. The grand-mother of the house. They couldnae bury their dead for the illness that swept through the family. It left no adult alive you see to do the digging.'

'But I thought…'

'No adult alive.'

Cal stared at her and then back at the dirty tinkers in the barge.

'What happened to the Russian?'

'What Russian would that be now?'

'The Russian that brought the smallpox to the family.'

'Och, who knows? Probably sailed away wi the fish.'

'I thought…' But there was no point in asking for more. Cal had already learned from listening to the emigrants at Leith that such stories weren't told with any particular attention to beginning, middle and end. In fact they weren't told as if they were stories at all. They were relayed as disjointed memories – back to front and jumbled with irrelevancies. Cal sighed.

'Ah, never mind.'

'Aye, it's a fine place is Rhue,' the old woman muttered. She patted Cal and he felt her claw-like fingers through his sleeve.

What if the whole country was blighted with disease? What then? Should he just abandon his plans to find passage to Lewis? Should he go ashore now and await the return steamer to Glasgow? Wouldn't that be a better idea than risking his health in this damp and disease-ridden land? *An bata dearg* – the red barge, with its tinkers. Perhaps he'd made a mistake coming to this country. A big mistake. Half the time he couldn't understand what people were saying to him and the other half they couldn't understand him.

Shaking the old woman off, Cal pushed through the crowd and stepped up to the gap in the rail. The woman with the baby had one hand on the rope ladder and was trying to step up to the deck above, but was being pushed back by one of the crew who was shouting at her in Gaelic.

Cal tried to get this man's attention but he was ignored.

Cal shouted: 'Excuse me.' Again, silence. He tried once more and this time the crewman spun round and shoved Cal back, at one and the same time knocking the woman with the baby off the ladder. She flailed in mid-air before falling back into the barge. The baby screamed, and the men below started up the ladder to have it out with the bully of a crewman.

The bargeman, realising that a riot was about to break out, slipped the line to *Clansman* and began to pull on the oars as hard as he could. The tinkers were left hanging in mid-air and dropped one by one into the ever-opening black space between ferry and barge, but the crewman's attention was turned wholly on Cal now. He shoved him against the outside cabin wall and stabbed the newspaperman's chest with a thick index finger.

'There's no getting off and there's no getting on. Can you no understand English?' Cal felt the crewman punch the words home.

He nodded swiftly, tightened his grasp on his flask and squeaked: 'Would you take a drink with me?' The crewman scowled for a moment. Cal searched for the right words.

'A wee dram,' he said at last and raised the flask at one and the same time remembering that it was empty.

A broad grin broke out on the crewman's face.

'Well now, there's an idea. Aye. I'll take a wee dram wi you.' He stepped back and Cal breathed a sigh of relief. Perhaps now would not be a good time to jump ship. Perhaps he would be better advised to just go along with things for now.

'Ah. Well now, I seem to have run out, but I have a full bottle of the finest in my luggage if you'll accompany me.'

The crewman stepped forward menacingly, but Cal was in his stride now. He knew how to bribe a man with drink.

'You have it all if you've a mind to let me be.' He gestured for the crewman to lead the way.

'Is that so?'

Cal smiled his agreement. Oh the demon drink, what you could buy with alcohol.

Later, Cal couldn't remember when he'd been so sick. He hugged the rails and wished he were dead. He hadn't reckoned on the crossing being quite so rough. He'd watched the belligerent crewman down his booze, wondering all the while whether he could make it through the voyage to his next drink. When the crewman had finally passed out Cal felt safe enough to go on deck, but by now the ship was lurching wildly through the waves. Cal had sunk to his knees and vomited, every nauseous moment feeling as if it was the first time he'd ever thrown up.

The *Clansman* ploughed through the Sea of the Hebrides, rounded Dunvegan Head on the Isle of Skye and forged a passage through the treacherous waters of the Little Minch. Here the wind blew strong across the hills of North Uist, and the currents that swirled in the Sound of Harris, between the more southerly isles of the Hebrides and Harris itself, confused those of the sea proper so that the steamer bucked and tossed in the dangerous waters.

Cal staggered across the deck. Pressing his cold wet face against the glass of a porthole he heard a comforting hum of voices. Why had he come here at all? What was it all for? A story? A far-fetched idea about lighthouses? He scrabbled inside his breast pocket for the all-important list. Was it still there? It had to be. It was all for naught if he'd lost the second list. Feeling the paper snug against his chest he relaxed slightly. He'd try to write something in the morning.

God, but it was cold, cold, and he shivered and pulled his sodden jacket tight around him. Standing there on deck, weathering the worst of the storm, he had a strange feeling that the steamer was some living entity doing battle with the forces of nature. He slid down the wall and huddled against it as the waves washed the deck in monotonous succession.

*

Joe's exhalations frosted the silence. A low fog covered the island, the darkness intense. Ice cut through to his bones, freezing his marrow. Fogbound in the darkness, he stood in the lee of the building with his back to the wall, breathing the very thickness of the air. Its surface pressed hard against his spine. There were other buildings on this island, buildings that had once housed men such as him. There was nothing there now. Nothing. The fog had erased everything. The night had swallowed the island whole and the fog took the remaining trace of earth and rocks right down to within two feet of Joe's body. He thought he could hear the roosting seabirds on the cliffs calling faintly to one another through the impenetrable night. He fixed on this sound hoping to find comfort in it, but it only made him feel even more nervous – and then the light cut through the pitch dark, illuminating the fog's blind grey mass, sweeping through and over the island and out into the sea beyond. Ghostly tendrils of water vapour reached out, as if a thousand spirits encircled the terrified lighthouse keeper, just waiting for the right moment to pluck him from the wall and wring the life out of him. The vapour caressed his face and curled round his legs like ivy colonising a forgotten statue. Then the light was gone, the night thick and black once more. Although the light rotated every thirty seconds it seemed much longer.

Joe wanted to close his eyes but was frozen rigid. The dark thickness of fog held his gaze and wouldn't let him shut it out. If there was nothing out there save the seabirds why was he so afraid? What was it about this nothing that scared him so? Why not go inside and warm himself by the fire? He must shrug off these morbid thoughts.

The blood pumped cold in his veins. Why not take me too? And in an instant he took it back. The icy air bit into his mind. He was frozen with both fear and cold, but with fear most of all.

Joe hadn't wanted to come back to the island after he'd reported the men's disappearance to Captain Harvie. He knew he had no choice but he hadn't wanted to do it. At first, it seemed as if he could cope. After the ship had left for Lewis he'd found something to do for just a while that stopped the mad thoughts from crowding his mind. He checked the oil and the wick. He lit the lamp and wrote up the log. He showed each of the men left with him how to make the half-hourly maintenance checks on the light and the machinery, and what to do if there was a problem.

They had a fire to set in the grate and brought coal in from the store. They made a pot of tea and Alan Macdonald poured a wee dram of whisky into Joe's cup and made him drink it down. There was more than enough to keep them all busy for the rest of the day, and they divided up the time into watches. Joe had shown them how the watch system worked: duty periods divided up on a rota that repeated every three days. They cast lots and Joe took the first watch at 20.00 hours, with Archie taking over at midnight. For their part Archie, Macdonald and Campbell walked in circles around Joe, unsure of themselves, unable to say anything about the missing men, and confused by their predicament. They were sailors after all and they found it strange to be marooned on this tiny island.

When Archie came on duty at midnight Joe retired to his bunk, but relieved of his duties he found he couldn't sleep – and if he was honest he hadn't even tried. He knew it was no use. The dreams, more powerful than ever now, would only have swamped him. He was afraid to close his eyes for more than a blink. Instead he excused himself and went outside. He wanted to check on the chickens. It was the one job they'd forgotten to do apart from tracking down the small flock of sheep, which were in any case more than capable of looking after themselves and frequently huddled beside the derelict chapel. The chickens were a different matter. No one had thought to feed them. They could all be dead – would all be dead. No point in checking really, but Joe did it anyway; glad to be on his own.

He took a small oil lamp with him, holding it high to illuminate the path, but he hadn't reckoned on it being quite so foggy. He felt his way slowly; cutting the corner at the rear of the lighthouse and coming on the coop sooner than if he followed the path to its end. He hung the lamp from a nail on the side of the coop and opened the gate. Treading softly on feathers his boot came up against the frozen body of a dead chicken. Taking the lamp down from the nail he held it high while he unlatched the wooden door. He didn't need to look inside, the smell told him everything. It had been eleven days since the men had disappeared, if the log was to be believed. The chickens had been without food and water for all that time. He would have to come back in the morning and clean it out.

The beacon flashed its warning out to sea and cast a pale light as it swept past the chickens and the scrubby garden that sometimes held potatoes and sometimes nothing but weeds. Joe was about to close the gate when a compulsion to count the bodies came over him. He couldn't explain why. Reaching inside with a gloved hand, he felt the cold lifeless bodies of the birds one by one. There were ten stiff little corpses. One at his feet made eleven. Where was the twelfth? There were twelve chickens. He scanned the inside of the run and then counted again, extending his right arm fully inside the coop and pressing his face against the outside wall so that the rough wood cut into his face. His fingers found feathers, beaks, claws, eggs, straw and then the twelfth chicken wedged between the rear boards and the end of the box. He brushed it lightly and it was then that he realised that it was still alive. Even through the thickness of his glove he could feel the life in its scrawny body. Ignoring the putrid smell he stuck his head and shoulders through the door and reached out for the survivor, taking it in both hands and pulling it close to his chest. It was barely alive, just barely. Outside the coop Joe opened his coat and tucked the bird inside. He thought he might feel better about himself if he could save this bird's life.

Standing now, back to the lighthouse wall, he wondered how he had come to be here. One moment he had been carrying the chicken back along the path, feeling its faintly beating heart through the thickness of his jersey and shirt against his chest, and the next he had been overwhelmed with fear. Light-headed, he stumbled and dropped the lamp, clutching his chest instinctively to prevent the chicken from being hurt if he fell. With the light extinguished he found he couldn't move. They were out there lying in wait – the demons of the night, the demons that lived on this island.

At least the lighthouse was real. At least he could feel it at his back. All he had to do was shuffle along the wall, turn the corner, open the door and go inside. If he could muster the strength of will he could even walk normally around the lighthouse, ignoring the evil that reached out for him, but he couldn't and instead stood, frozen with both fear and cold. The light swept round and Joe followed its path with his eyes. The beam, as strong as it was, gave off only the briefest of light this close to the lighthouse. It was out there in the Atlantic that the beacon's brightness could be viewed at its strongest; a caution for passing ships to beware of the rocks.

Fastening on the thought that Archie wasn't a lighthouse keeper but only a sailor, and not used to tending the lamp and keeping watch, Joe inched sideways as if on a narrow ledge atop a tall building where one false step would send him plummeting to his death. He had the chicken to think of after all. It had suffered enough. He thought briefly that it would have been kinder just to wring its neck and leave it with its companions, but it was too late for that now. If he saved its life perhaps he would in turn be saved. When the next sweep of the light passed Joe closed his eyes against the snarling ghosts beyond the fog and, keeping his left hand on the wall and his right cupped under the chicken inside his jacket, he made out along the side of the lighthouse until he came to the corner. Opening his eyes he could see the door outlined vaguely black as the light moved on to the far side of the island. Just a short distance now and he would be inside. Focusing on the door, he made a beeline for it before his courage gave out, not pausing to glance behind at what might be following.

Archie Lamont looked up from his book, his eyes flicking over Joe as he entered the kitchen.

'You should be away to your bed, lad. It's a powerful cold night to be gadding about in.'

Joe unbuttoned his coat and carefully lifted the chicken out.

'God help us. What is it you've got there?'

The chicken was the scrawniest thing he'd ever laid eyes on.

'It's the only one left alive,' said Joe meekly.

'Aye, and I've no wonder. It's no fit even for the pot.'

Joe pulled a drawer out from the chest and emptied the contents.

'You're no thinking of saving it, are you?'

'Would you have me wring its neck?'

'Aye lad. That would be best. Put it out of its misery.'

'I cannae do that,' and Joe made a newspaper nest inside the drawer, put the chicken in and placed the whole thing next to the fire.

'Och, you're off your head if you think it'll last the night.'

Joe ran a little water into a saucer and put it in the drawer close enough to the bird that it could take some if it wanted without straining. Then, remembering that the chicken hadn't eaten in days, he ran into the storeroom and grabbed a handful of grain from a sack stacked against the far wall. He spread the grain on the newspaper in the drawer and stood back to admire his handiwork. Archie Lamont looked on, scratching his head and shaking it.

'I cannae see what use it is. I just cannae see it. You should get some sleep. You need it.'

'Will you no keep an eye on it for me?' Joe asked.

'I'm here until the next watch.'

'I'd be very grateful.'

Archie patted Joe on the shoulder and smiled.

'Go get some shut-eye lad. You'll feel better come morning so you will.'

Joe sighed. He felt so guilty for being alive. For not having been with his fellow keepers when they were taken in death. Yet he was scared beyond belief of the black hand of death and still couldn't bring himself to lie down and close his eyes.

'I reckon I'll go up to and look at the lamp. Did you wind the weights?'

'I've been up not ten minutes ago.'

'I'll go again.'

The door slammed hard on its hinges.

Climbing the stairs in the dark, Joe trailed one hand on the wall as the spiral wound upwards, avoiding the brass handrail because to touch it would mean he would have to polish it later. It was cold in this void and his footsteps echoed. Stepping out into the gallery, he observed the light kindly, noticing how it was fractured a thousand times by the surrounding prisms. Standing in front of it he let it bathe him with the warmth it gave off. Up here like this he couldn't see anything outside; couldn't hear anything either, save for the constant roll of the sea over the gentle whine of the lantern's machinery and the soft hum of luminescence. It was as if he had become invisible. And in his invisibility, Joseph Moore found safety for the first time since landing on the island.

*

Mairi found Cal slumped on a bench in the early hours of the morning. The sea had stilled, the Lewis coast briefly visible in the distance. Dawn blessed the sky with a luminous glow in the east, though daylight proper was still many hours away.

She lowered her tired bones onto the bench and wiped Cal's wet face with the sleeve of her tattered coat. The newspaperman woke with a start, gasping at the coldness of the air and the eerie calm that had descended with the passing of the storm. He pushed Mairi's arm away roughly.

'You shouldnae be out here in the cold, laddie. Come wi me into the warm. Come on now. Let Mairi take care o you the now.'

Cal shook his head. He didn't want to go inside. He wanted to stay right here.

He mumbled: 'Leave me be.'

'There's the lights o Lewis, there,' Mairi announced, pointing to the shoreline where a few brief specks of lamp-light shone dim.

Cal lunged out at her and staggered to the rail where the water washed gently now against the steamer's hull. A soft spray dampened his face.

'Where are we?'

'There's Cromore o'er there. It'll no be long now and you'll be stepping ashore at Stornoway.'

Cal felt the bile rise in his throat and he spat into the sea.

'You'll feel better when you're on dry land. Aye, you'll feel better then. And if you've a mind I'll take you to my own wee house and you can sup wi me the while. Get your bearings. Aye, that would be grand for ye.'

'Shut up.' Cal felt the world dive away from him. He had to get rid of this old crone.

'But…'

'Shut up with your yabbering on.' Her voice sounded like a seagull's caw, constantly squawking into the wind. He couldn't take anymore of it. Not after the night he'd had. Not now, not ever.

'Well I...'

'Shut up,' Cal shouted. 'Shut up,' and he lunged for her across the deck, sending her poor crumpled body sprawling as his fists lashed out at her ragged shape.

Mairi cowered for a few moments and then crawled away from him. Cal sank to his knees, his whole body shaking with rage. He spread his hands out in fear, watching them dance, and for the first time in his life wished he didn't drink.

At the cabin wall Mairi drew herself up, cast a look of absolute hatred towards Cal and cursed in the filthiest Gaelic she could bring to her lips, damning the poor newspaperman to hell.

SEVEN

❧

Thursday, 27th December

The weather changed little overnight, but by the following morning the atmosphere inside the lighthouse was tense with unspoken sentiment. The four men walked circles round each other, avoiding conversation, avoiding each other's eyes, avoiding the very thing that was on each man's mind. Although Joe was used to the intimate nature of a lighthouse, he felt as if he'd spilt his thoughts into the ominous silence and now there was no escape. Every bone in his body ached from lack of sleep, from raw emotion, but mostly from the fear he held close to his heart. Perhaps if his father had been there he might have understood, but Joe's father was long dead, drowned at sea, or so they said.

Joe had only been fourteen and his father's passing had hit him hard. Just when he needed him the most, just when Joe was himself becoming a man, Joseph senior had disappeared from his son's life. The love the boy felt for the man became a gaping hole of fear; a wound. If his father had been here he would have listened to his son and understood what the boy was going through, but the boy was a man now – had to act like a man and swallow his tears in order to present a brave face to the world. Wasn't that what men did?

Joe peered through the window and tried to see if he could make out the path.

'The chicken died, laddie.' Archie threw Joe a look of apology. 'I told you as much.'

'I'm going out,' Joe announced, wanting to escape the close confines of the lighthouse. He had always liked the cosiness of this kitchen but now it seemed like a prison, the evidence of the three missing men still surrounded them: the remaining oilskin and boots, the logbook, the plates the men had eaten off, the cups they drank from. It was like living in a mausoleum. Perhaps outside he'd feel better. He slammed the door as he went out, trying to work out what he felt so angry about. Perhaps it was death itself that angered him – the unfairness of it, taking people when they were least ready for it.

When Joe's father had died they'd buried an empty casket, there being no body to inter. Joe's mother hadn't known whether to throw a handful of soil down into the grave or not. She held onto the black mass until it was mud in her hands. When Joe turned to her later she had soil-streaked cheeks where she'd rubbed her eyes with those hands, and rivulets of sorrow had coursed her face. He wanted to wipe her tears away but he was afraid of his mother's anguish. It seemed too raw to deal with. He wished with all his heart then that his father would come home and that everything would be back the way it was, but it never happened. A yawning gulf of separation opened up between Joe and his mother. Although she never recovered from the loss of her husband, she never again bared her emotions in front of her son. She hid all behind an implacable wall of silence. It was as if a man's life had not just ended prematurely, it had never been at all. Thus, in losing his father, Joseph Moore lost his mother too.

Joe walked in a grey world down to the west landing and stood at the top of the steps leading down the cliff-face. If his father had just come home he thought he would know how to handle the emptiness he felt now. All at once he let out a shout that was immediately swallowed by the blank face of fog that swirled at the precipice's edge. A light breeze had risen from the sea and the air was layered with cotton-white eddies that now parted, now closed again. Joe took one step down and felt the weight of his years settling on him as if he was a hundred and not the young man he knew himself to be. The sea broke foam over the rocks below. He could hear it now when he listened, when he took his ear away from the voices inside his head that spoke to him of his weakness and his fears. He trained that ear on the crash of the sea and felt the world dip away from him.

The handrail broke his fall. He grabbed it tight and steadied himself as the dizzy spell passed. Blue sky parted the mist and out on the horizon the cresting waves shone silver.

How could there be such beauty in this pain? How could it be that the world still spun on its axis and that the sun still rose in the heavens each morning? How could it be that a man's life could be taken so easily with no explanation?

Joe took another step down, holding the railing tight. He intended to go to the sea's edge, where it sucked ferociously at the landing stage, but he noticed that the handrail was warped and twisted on its mountings. Forgetting his previous nervousness, he now inspected the metal, noting how the upright had been wrenched clean from its concrete base. Reading these signs gave him back a sense of control and he wondered what kind of force it would have needed to twist the metal like this. He took the steps down to the water's edge, noticing that the box containing the mooring ropes and tackle was upturned. When he lifted it there were neither ropes inside nor any to be seen strewn over the rocks or down the cliff-face. Little else seemed out of place. Putting the box back where he'd found it, he made his way carefully down the remaining steps to the bottom where the waves washed angrily against the granite. The vast Atlantic rolled towards Eilean Mor, the waves magnified now by Joe's proximity to the water. He scowled as the spray hit him in the face, listening to the surf echoing around the cliffs, to the sea birds calling to one another, and to the wind. And there in the distance, piercing the murmur of the sea, perhaps just beyond the curve of the cliffs, came another sound – that of babies crying.

Joe flashed frightened eyes in the direction of this noise and listened for the crying a second time. It came faintly, as if being carried away from him, but the thought of this terrified him all the more. He clapped his hands over his ears, but now the infants cried all the louder and the sound bled in through his palms as if the action of shutting it out had in fact magnified it. Logic told him it was only the seals; that although he couldn't see them they were there beyond the next ridge of cliffs, but for all that his rational mind tried to make sense of the noise his unconscious mind twisted and warped the sound until he couldn't stand it any more. He sank to his knees at the water's edge, the waves washing over him, the spray stinging his eyes until he was sightless from the salty pain. Still the cries came. And they weren't babies that cried now but human voices, for Hebridean men thought that seals were the souls of those drowned at sea and Joe believed this with a passion, even though reason screamed that it was only the seals.

Only the seals.

And even as he knelt there on the bottom step of the landing stage it came to him that his own drowned father could be one of this company of seals and that all might still be well if he could only find him. With this thought now uppermost in his mind Joe scrambled back up the steps, the waves still lashing tendrils of foam at his feet. Over the top of the cliff and around the rocks, and the seals were clearly visible now on the granite below, their bodies camouflaged somewhat by the greyness of stone. Joe lowered himself to the first jutting shelf. The sea swirled dangerously below him, and the seals still cried dolefully. Joe made his way down the cliff-face; slipping here and there, his fingers finding crevices, his toes scrabbling against the rocks. One-by-one the seals slid clumsily into the sea, transforming themselves into graceful mermaid-like creatures whose pleading doe eyes begged Joe to follow them, for here was a realm of fluidity unlike any other – a watery landscape of ever-changing wonder.

Desperate to find the seal that carried his father's soul, Joe shouted at the seaborne creatures, wildly waving his arms: 'I'm here. Wait. Don't leave me. Wait.' But it was no use. The seals disappeared beneath the waves. With their departure the surf rang loud as if there was no other sound in the entire world save the breaking waters on the rocks of this little island. Joe sat down at the water's edge and allowed the waves to wash over him. If he was to die then best it be here, following his father into the deep beyond.

It seemed like hours before Joe came to his senses. He was still alive. His father hadn't returned to claim him for his own. The seals were gone for today. The fellow keepers, his friends, had passed away. Dead. Washed out to sea or taken by some mighty force. And suddenly the feeling that he was not alone came over Joe so that he stood up and turned, his back to the sea, in order to climb up the cliff-face, to shake off the feeling of being watched by an unseen force. Perhaps it's God, he thought. But he'd never had that much time for the Almighty. Oh, he prayed. He asked for deliverance from his fears, always his fears, but without real fervour – without real belief. And he wondered, as he scaled the heights, if renewing his acquaintance with God in a church might bring him relief from this nightmare – might show him why the men had been taken.

*

At some time during the previous night the temperature had dropped enough that a thin film of ice formed on the steps leading up to 84 George Street. As the first of the staff arrived at the Northern Lighthouse Board's headquarters this ice caused some consternation. Ordinarily the boy would have already been sent out to sprinkle salt on the steps and thus prevent any accidents. This morning though the boy was occupied running messages between Secretary William Murdoch and the telegraph office. The 'boy' was a young man of seventeen, Robbie Macfee, employed by the NLB to undertake such menial tasks. He was not the same boy who had delivered the sad tidings of the lighthouse keepers' disappearance to Murdoch the evening before.

There was also ice on the inside of the windows in Murdoch's office. Once the fire was lit in the grate the ice turned slowly to water. Robbie watched a trickle of condensation on the windowpane, his mind wandering as usual.

'These need to be sent as soon as possible. Do you understand?' Murdoch glanced over the rim of his glasses, a clutch of papers in his hand. The boy was truly in a world of his own.

'Macfee!' bellowed Murdoch

Robbie sprang to attention and took the papers.

'It's vitally important that you don't lose any of those on the way.' Murdoch pushed back his chair, stood up and took off his glasses, toying with them thoughtfully as he walked over to the window where the condensation now pooled on the sill below.

Gazing at the magnificence of the Georgian façade on the building across the road he said: 'Wait for the replies and bring them to me at once. Do not get sidetracked, mind.'

He waved his glasses at Robbie, who shuffled the papers but didn't move.

'Well? What are you waiting for?' he shouted.

Robbie took off, slamming the office door behind him with such force that the condensation bounced off the sill and dripped onto Murdoch's shoes. He turned back to his desk and cleared the papers from it in one fell swoop, scattering them disconsolately onto the floor. Head in hands, he pondered his problem. A nightmare had ensued that would need explaining at the next meeting of the Commissioners. Meanwhile the investigation must be undertaken at once without hindrance. With any luck Superintendent Robert Muirhead, the best man the NLB had in Murdoch's opinion, was already on his way north to meet the mail steamer at Oban. Oh how Murdoch wished that he could unravel this mystery himself, but it could not be so. He couldn't go. He had other duties; duties that saw him deskbound, forever writing notes, forever reporting to the Commissioners.

Telegrams sent on 27th December 1900 at 11.00am

To Master, Hesperus, Braescleit, Calanais

Remain Braescleit. Milne – Tiumpanhead and Jack, Assistant Storekeeper will arrive tomorrow night or Saturday morning to take charge of Flannans. You can then bring Macdonald and your two men away while you await at Braescleit.

Secretary

To Ferrier, Lightkeeper, Stornoway

Call on Occasional and proceed to Tiumpanhead today for fortnight. Milne goes to Flannans in consequence of accident there. Wire reply.

Secretary

To Milne, Tiumpanhead Lighthouse, Portnaguran

*Accident Flannan Isles. You go there and take charge for fort-
night or so. Meet mail steamer, Stornoway tomorrow night. Jack,
Assistant Storekeeper will arrive with her. Drive over together to
Braescleit and join the Hesperus. Ferrier, Stornoway will arrive
tonight to take charge, Tiumpanhead. Wire reply.*

Secretary

*

'And what of the whalers? Do you no ken they took the
men?' It was Campbell who spoke. The three sailors huddled
around the kitchen fire watching the thick grey smoke curl
up the chimney. They were used to each other's company but
not to the permanence of this landlocked gloryhole out in
the wild Atlantic.

'It's wet that coal. That's the trouble.' Archie drew
breath, knocking his pipe out on the grate before he went on,
'And what would the whalers be wanting wi three cussed
lighthouse men?'

'I'm just saying. If you're looking for an answer it's
staring you in the face. Those whalers have caused trouble
afore and they'll cause it again.'

'Not here. If they'd have landed on the island there'd be
mention in the log book, and there is none.'

'They didnae have time to write it down, man. They
were taken hostage.'

Macdonald looked surprised. 'Och, what for? There's
no reason to take three lighthouse keepers hostage. They
need the lighthouse. They work these waters same as you and
I. No self-respecting seaman in his right mind is going to
take a lighthouse man hostage.'

Campbell shook his head.

'They're Harris men those whalers. They bear a grudge easily they do.'

Narrowing his eyes Archie considered for a moment before replying: 'Aye. A grudge. It's a thought, but I'm no convinced.'

'I reckon it would be easy for a Harris man to bear a grudge. A Harris whaler even easier,' said Campbell.

'No. You're wrong.' Macdonald got up and crossed to the window, looking out on the bleak wet landscape and sea beyond. 'We all signed the visitors' book when we landed. And I went through it. A year's worth of visitors. Not one mention of a whaler landed at this island. Every single person that's landed is written in that book,' and here he pointed to the visitors' book on the shelf. 'And not one single mention of a whaler come to visit.'

'He's right. I have to say he's right,' Archie said to Campbell.

'I've seen them wi my own eyes,' Campbell argued. 'They sail between Rockall and St Kilda and here. And you cannae tell me any different.'

'Aye,' said Macdonald. 'But the whaling season is between April and October. They don't sail these waters in December. Not even for a grudge.'

'I've heard tell they catch as far away as the Faroes,' Archie ruminated, not giving Campbell's theory of a whaler bearing a grudge against the lighthouse keepers much credence.

'But the whale goes south like the birds when the days shorten. I've seen the Nordkapers and Sperm. No so many o them Humpbacks though.'

'Och whales. It's harder than the fishing that is. Have you no seen them dragged up the causeway at Bun Abhainn-eadar?'

'I've no seen them. Aren't Norwegians running that whaling station?' asked Archie.

'Norwegians. Now what's a Norwegian doing wi a grudge against a lighthouse man. Tell me that,' and Macdonald shook his head angrily at Campbell.

'It's isnae my fault they went and got themselves taken,' Campbell replied. 'I'd have put up more o a fight if it was me. There wasn't nothing but a chair upturned. What kind o man lets himself be taken by Norwegians?'

Macdonald grabbed his oilskin off the peg.

'I'm no going to listen to this. Are you going listen to this?' he asked Archie. 'Are you no coming with me? Leave the barm pot to himself.'

'I might at that,' replied Archie.

Campbell grunted, 'Where's the laddie gone?'

Archie shrugged. 'Young Joseph? Taking it hard that one.'

'We should be out there,' said Macdonald. 'Find the laddie and sort this thing out for him. Set his mind straight afore someone tells him about Norwegian whalers,' and he looked pointedly at Campbell.

'Maybe you're right,' agreed Archie. 'I'll come with you. If the lad comes back you can tell him where we are,' he said to Campbell. 'It's your watch anyway, isn't it?'

Campbell hunched closer to the fire.

'Aye, that's right. Leave me behind wi the ghosts.'

The two sailors stepped outside the lighthouse, fastened their oilskins and pulled their woollen hats low over their brows against the cold. The fog had almost dissipated and the world had taken on a misty impermanence that shifted ghost-like as they walked.

'It's no the whalers that took them,' Macdonald said quietly, more to himself than Archie.

'No,' was all his companion said by way of reply.

They crossed the rails of the track that spanned the distance between the landing stages and the lighthouse, walking now towards the western landing stage.

'Have you heard o the Phantom o the Seven Hunters?' Macdonald said suddenly, pulling up short. The rails connected to the west landing stage were wrenched clean from their stanchions. Macdonald nodded towards them. 'And what manner of thing could do that I ask you?'

Archie traced the track down to the cliff's edge noting where the rails had broken clean in two before speaking.

'Something mighty powerful.'

'Did you ever hear o the Phantom o the Seven Hunters?' Macdonald asked again.

'What's this superstition? And you quick to dismiss Campbell and his whalers.'

'Did you hear of it?' Macdonald said again, more agitated than before.

'Aye. I heard,' replied Archie angrily. 'But it's no more likely than Norwegians and that's a fact. Don't let that laddie hear you talking like this. Whalers is one thing but phantoms, that's another thing entirely.'

'When I took on wi the *Hesperus* they joked about the Phantom o the Seven Hunters. I gave it no mind, but I'm not so sure now.' Macdonald cast about for a loose rock to hurl down into the sea below the landing. Both men listened as the rock bounced on the cliff-face; an echoing almost hollow before it was swallowed by the surf.

Macdonald went on: 'The Phantom. I remember them saying it was a shape-shifter…'

'That watched over the Flannans and was greatly displeased by the intrusion o the lighthouse men,' finished Joe as he walked up behind them. Archie smiled and clapped a hand on Joe's arm giving it a welcoming shake.

'Don't pay him any mind. Where've you been, laddie? We've been worried about you.'

'Walking. Just walking.'

'Have you found anything?'

'Only what you see here. The tackle's gone, but the ropes are down there on the rocks. The crane's in one piece, but look see… the handrails are twisted and the tracks are broken.' Joe led Archie and Macdonald down the steps of the west landing, showing them what he'd discovered earlier that day.

'Nothing else to see. I've walked the island over. Nothing. No sign of a struggle. No blood,' and here he opened his hand and looked hard at it as if expecting to see blood well up in his palm and overflow onto the ground. Archie watched Joe momentarily and then took the hand Joe held outstretched and clamped his own over it.

'No more talk of blood… or phantoms,' Archie said, and he wagged his head at Macdonald. 'What o the east landing?'

Joe pulled his hand free from Archie's, stuffing it in his pocket before glancing eastward.

'We landed there. There's nothing to see. It happened here. Whatever it was. This is the place.'

'And the rest o the island? You said there's nothing. There's an old bothy on yon rocks. Am I no right?'

'On the headland, Mal nam Both. They call the place Bothan Chlann 'ic Phail. There's a Teampull and two other buildings. All ruins. It's this way if you want to see them.'

A few minutes later the three men came up against a low wall that separated the ruined buildings from the rest of the island.

'What was it?' asked Macdonald, resting a foot up on the wall and leaning an elbow on his knee, cupping his head in the palm of his hand.

'Monks lived here,' said Joe. He didn't like this place.

'Aye. A monastery. Chapel and two cells. See?' Archie climbed the ruined wall and slapped his hand against the stones of the Teampull.

'St Flannan, wouldn't you say, laddie?' He grinned at Joe. 'I'd make a good monk me. No women to boss you about.'

'You've been at sea too long,' said Macdonald and he jumped the wall and entered one of the cells. It was roofless and built of dry stone walling.

He said: 'Och well, it's no different to a hundred old houses back on the mainland.'

'It's old though,' said Joe. 'Older than the houses.' He was the only one of them that hadn't crossed the wall to the consecrated ground beyond. Now he began to back off as if he'd seen something and wanted away from the place.

'St Flannan died in the eighth century,' he said.

'How do you know?' asked Macdonald.

'I read about it, and I asked when I came here first. He was the son of the King Turlough of Thomond, in

Ireland. We should go back now,' he said, turning suddenly and beginning to walk away fast. 'You've left Campbell on his own. He's no the experience.'

Archie called out: 'You havenae told us about this Flannan.'

Joe stopped in his tracks and turned back. He just wanted to be indoors now. He thought it was strange that his mood had turned so since the morning, when he couldn't wait to get outside. He sighed before answering Archie.

'Flannan was sent to live with a man called Blathmet who was a renowned teacher.'

'And this Blathmet lived here?' Macdonald asked.

'No,' Joe continued. 'I don't know. Flannan became a monk at a place called Killaloe. He was a baker.'

'A baker and a monk?' Archie frowned.

'They had to eat.'

Archie nodded. 'Go on.'

'We should go back.'

'Finish the tale, laddie.'

'He'd been baking for all of thirty-six hours when a heavenly light shone through the fingers of his left hand.'

'Is that a fact?' Macdonald whistled. 'Thirty-six hours straight. That's enough to set any man's hands alight.'

'You're no taking this serious,' Archie scolded. 'Listen to the laddie. Finish the tale, Joe.'

'Och well. There's no much more to tell. The light lit up the darkness and Flannan could carry on baking.'

'Seems right and proper for a lighthouse to have the name of a man wi light coming out o his hand.'

'He went to Rome,' continued Joe.

'Are you a Catholic then, laddie?' asked Macdonald.

'No, I am not.'

'Only it just seems you know a lot about this Flannan here. If you're no a Catholic then what are you?' Macdonald cast a threatening look in Joe's direction.

'I'm nothing. I just read it that's all.'

Archie came to Joe's defence. 'Och, away wi you now, Alan. He's a storyteller. Let him tell it.'

'I just read it. There's no more to tell. I don't know if the Irish Flannan is this Flannan. An Irishman might tell you different.'

'Aye, an Irishman's a Catholic too,' Macdonald sneered and began to walk back towards the lighthouse. 'Are you no an Irishman?'

'Dinnae take any notice o him, laddie,' Archie said to Joe as they followed in Macdonald's footsteps. 'He's got it in his head that there's a phantom running around here and you've put the fear o God in him, that's all.' Archie chuckled.

Joe said nothing. He was remembering the old tale about the phantom of the isles. What if it was true? What if the phantom was the ghost of the former inhabitants? He knew that the land had been owned once by the Macphail family, who kept sheep here on Eilean Mor and who lived for a while at least on the second biggest island, Eilean Tighe. He wasn't sure about the story of St Flannan. He'd read about him years ago before he'd joined the NLB. He wasn't sure if what he'd said was right. Perhaps this was where Flannan himself had lived. He shuddered at the thought and glanced at Archie for reassurance.

'Are you alright, laddie?'

'Aye. I suppose. I just don't like it out here much.'

He quickened his step and was pleased when he could feel beneath his feet the solidity of the paving that led up to the lighthouse door.

*

In summer, the railway track north to Crianlarich, where from Tarbet onwards it skirts Loch Lomond, is verdant. It teeters precariously at times on a rocky cut beside the cold waters of the tree-fringed loch, making it hard for passengers travelling by rail to glimpse the waters below without experiencing vertigo. On this cold winter's day the loch was almost invisible from the train, an icy mist wreathing the bare tree trunks such that the tops of the trees seemed to emerge ethereally from the world at the water's edge.

Superintendent Robert Muirhead gazed blindly out of the window at the obscured loch. His well-worn tweeds lent him the air of a ghillie, and he 'wore' his pipe rather than smoked it. Chewing on the stem now he pondered how long it would take him to reach his destination. It would be another few hours yet before he disembarked from the train at Connel Ferry, itself some five miles from his destination of Oban, where he would catch the mail steamer out to Lewis. With any luck he could be on the island by the following morning. That would make it 28th December. If the two men he'd arranged to meet at Stornoway arrived on schedule they could all travel out to the Flannans together. If not, well then he'd just have to play it by ear. He was good at that – playing it by ear. Years of watching the lights, the men, the weather, and the sea had endowed in him the ability to be flexible, to take things as they came. He was a shrewd judge of character and an even shrewder judge of the vagaries of nature. He'd get to the bottom of this mystery though it pained him to do so; pained him because he had a soft spot for the Flannans and yes, an even softer spot for the keepers themselves, two of whom he'd picked for the job himself. He wished he was returning to the island in better circumstances. He had only recently visited the keepers and renewed his friendship with James Ducat, whom he considered a credit to the NLB.

The train had left the lochside now and was gathering speed, the engine's smoke indistinguishable from the fog. Muirhead rested further back in his seat and closed his eyes. He'd been present at the lighting of the Flannan Isles lighthouse on the night of its installation: December 7th 1899, just over a year ago now. With him had been the District Superintendent John Smibert and three lighthouse keepers: James Ducat, Thomas Marshall and Angus McEachern, two of whom were now missing from their post. At the time of the first lighting Angus McEachern was on temporary duty at the Flannans from his usual post at Crimore, pending the arrival of a permanent keeper.

Those first few months at the new light had been busy ones for all concerned. There had been the weather to consider; often the tender couldn't make it at the appointed time because the sea was running high, and this state of affairs had not eased, and was not likely to improve with the passage of time. When the relief was late the men had to make do with what few stores they put aside for just such an eventuality. It was something the keepers were used to, no matter which light they were stationed at.

Getting to know one another was something else the keepers had to contend with. If you didn't get on then there was nowhere you could escape to when you were stationed on a rock or island lighthouse. But these men had known what was being asked of them – to abandon their families, if they had any, in order to live for three months in close companionship with two others before going onshore for a brief spell. In circumstances such as these the keepers learned when to avoid a man's gaze and when to hold their tongue. They knew when to draw one another out and when to talk of home. They knew which words would cause most pain and which would heal old wounds. It was as if they'd married the light and each other, and they kept the rules the Northern Lighthouse Board demanded of them just as surely as they kept their vows to wife and family waiting for them back at home. Not all had women to return to. Young Tommie Marshall for instance had no wife, but he was a Lewisman with an aged father and a younger sister to care for.

Muirhead was proud of 'his' men. He spent most of his time inspecting the lights around Scotland's shores and knew almost all the keepers personally. Although he spent weeks away from home sometimes he would take his wife along with him, as he had done on the recent visit to the Flannans.

Muirhead sighed. The thought that he was the last man to see the poor lost keepers alive played on his mind. What to do for the widow Ducat, and Marshall's father, not to mention Macarthur's wife, stranded in a foreign country, far from the place of her birth in the south of England. He supposed she would go back home now. No point in staying. She hadn't the Gaelic to stay among the locals, and didn't she have two children? So sad. So sad.

The fog outside the carriage window had all but dissipated and the train was taking a long slow curve, matching the contours of the rising hillside it was skirting. For a moment the engine was visible from Muirhead's carriage. The hypnotic motion of the train, the sound of the track passing beneath the wheels, the hiss and chug of the steam, the pistons working at full tilt, all served now to lull the Superintendent into a deep sleep, where he dreamed of the sea and a great sweeping light that illuminated all in its path.

EIGHT

❧

*E*xcept for their sojourn to the ruined chapel the men used what little daylight there was during the rest of the day to undertake routine duties, with top priority given to cleaning. The lantern panes and optical apparatus were polished until they shone brightly. The NLB maxim was: 'Constant vigilance and attention to details of Lightroom duty are required of Lightkeepers in order that the light may be kept at its maximum efficiency'.

While there was light to work by Joe kept himself and the others as busy as possible. For one thing it staved off the anxiety all were now suffering to various degrees, and for another it gave the men purpose. Once the evening began to close in though, there was little for anyone to do save for the man on watch. In more tranquil times Joe would read. He had a small collection of books stashed under his berth and didn't mind if others shared them while he was onshore, but since he'd told the story about St Flannan to Archie Lamont and Alan Macdonald he couldn't keep his mind from wandering over all the things he'd learned about the tiny group of islands. Some things he'd read, but mostly he'd gleaned the knowledge from locals on Lewis. Tall tales and folklore mostly, but he couldn't help believing it.

There were ruins of holy places all over it seemed. The Celtic priests were good at picking fertile ground on which to build their temples. After St Columba died in 597AD the monks left Iona and set about looking for places they could make their own. Many founded tiny hermitages on islands named for their bounty. But there were other tales more terrible than those of isolated monastic communities; stories about blood libations called t-ainmean, where the blood from the first animal of the slaughtering season was collected and then poured into the sea while a strange incantation was invoked. And then there were tales such as that of the old wizard of Holm, known as Fiosaiche Thuilm who it was said cast spells and used roots and herbs, stems and leaves to tie up the magic. All of these stories fascinated Joe, but they also scared him. He couldn't tell truth from fantasy and now they were all getting jumbled up in his mind so that the old monks were becoming wizards and the spells were becoming prayers.

Archie took the first four hours with Campbell following on after him. By the time Macdonald had taken his turn it was around four in the morning of 28th December. Joe had spent his time supervising; these men were not lighthouse keepers after all. If anything should go wrong, if the light should fail then none but him knew what to do to rectify the situation. Besides which he couldn't sleep. Every time he closed his eyes he saw the missing keepers, black-eyed and bloated, staring at him from the bottom of the sea. Left to himself Joe felt a continued presence with him, save when he stood in the gallery with the lamp shining its brightest, warming his back.

At around six o'clock, Joe opened the kitchen door and stood on the threshold, a cup of freshly brewed tea in his hand. It was misty outside but not so much as the day before; besides it was always misty here in the mornings. The sea sounded fierce against the island's rocky shore, but that was nothing new either. The darkness of the previous night still lay complicit with the horizon. There was a while yet before dawn, itself as late in winter as sunset was early. Joe sipped the tea and felt the weariness in his bones. It was as if he'd aged a thousand years in just a few short days. With barely any sleep in all that time he knew that sooner or later he would have to succumb to his weariness. Then he would be forced to face his night terrors head on. Yet really, he thought, would sleep be any different to this waking nightmare? Perhaps not. Once he'd enjoyed being a lighthouse keeper – once. But now? Now he wasn't so sure he wanted to wrestle with the evils his mind visited on him. Now he couldn't tell whether the darkness outside was the same as the darkness that came when he closed his eyes. It was getting so that waking, sleeping, breathing, talking and thinking were all one and the same thing – and it was all unremittingly evil, as if he'd been poisoned somehow. As if something was eating away at him. He wondered if there was some kind of wicked creature living inside him, torturing him.

A piercing shriek went up and he dropped the teacup on the step. Turning quickly he tried to close the kitchen door, his heart beating fast in his chest – only it wouldn't shut properly. In a panic he pushed hard, feeling something outside pushing against him. He braced himself on the wood, both palms flat. A scraping sound shuddered through the woodwork, but still the door wouldn't close. Terrified now, Joe barely felt the tears on his face he was so determined that whatever was outside wasn't coming in. It was not gaining entry. Whatever it was. Not even if he had to stand here forever and a day. The shriek went up again and just for a moment he froze. Just for a moment. Then he slammed hard against the door again and again.

'What in damnation's going on?' It was Archie. He stood in the gloom of the small storeroom scratching his head, his eyes still half-shut with sleep. Joe barely gave him a glance as the old sailor pressed a hand against the door. He hung his head between his arms his tears falling silently onto the stone floor.

'There's nothing outside, is there?' he hissed. 'Nothing. I'm going mad, aren't I?'

'Come on, laddie. Away to your bed now. I'll take over here.'

Joe allowed Archie to lead him back into the safety of the kitchen. The door remained shut. Nothing came crashing in.

'I cannae sleep. I don't want to sleep.' He cast a fearful glance back at the kitchen door before sitting down at the table and staring disconsolately into the fire.

'Is it the gannets that keep you awake? Och, but you've heard them before. They're all around here. They woke me. I hate them.' Archie almost spat the words out.

'Gannets?'

'Aye, gannets, or some such stupid bird. Was it that you were afraid of?'

'Aye, maybe.' But he wasn't sure, not sure at all that it was a mere bird making that fearful noise. Enough to wake the dead, Joe thought, but of course he had heard it before and deep inside knew the noise was only a bird.

'Shall I be taking a little looksee for you?'

'No.'

'Set your mind at rest,' Archie ventured.

'I said no.'

'Set mine at rest at any rate. You cannae be too sure those Norwegians won't creep up here and snatch us away just like they snatched away the others.'

'Norwegians?'

Archie opened the kitchen door. It made a horrifying scraping noise on the floor. He looked outside and shook his head.

'Anything?' Joe asked weakly.

'Nothing.' Archie bent over and picked up the broken teacup. 'Bit of china wedged under the door maybe.'

'Aye, china,' muttered Joe.

Now he felt a little calmer, he saw the senselessness of his fear. It had been the gannets and the broken teacup. That was all. There was nothing out there laying in wait for him. Nothing. It was like the other night. There'd been nothing after him then either.

'Go to bed, laddie. Be better for all if you sleep.'

'No. I've something I have to do.'

At a little past seven on the morning of 28th December 1900, Joseph Moore set the stone from his pocket on the table top, put pen to paper and wrote his report for the Northern Lighthouse Board and for Superintendent Robert Muirhead, who would soon be with them. Mostly though, Joe wrote the report for himself; to assuage his own feelings of helplessness and fear.

Joseph Moore's report to the Northern Lighthouse Board

Friday 28th December 1900

Sir, It is with deep regret I wish you to learn the very sad affair that has taken place here during the last fortnight, namely the disappearance of my two fellow lighthouse keepers, Mr Ducat and Mr Marshall, together with the Occasional Keeper, Donald Macarthur from this island. As you are aware a relief was made on the 26th. That day, as on other relief days, we came to anchorage under Flannan Islands and not seeing the Lighthouse Flag flying, we thought they did not perceive us coming. The steamer's horn was sounded several times, but still no reply. At last Captain Harvie deemed it prudent to lower a boat and land a man if it was possible. I was the first to land, leaving Mr Macormick and his men in the boat 'till I should return from the lighthouse.

I went up and on coming to the entrance gate I found it closed. I made for the entrance store room door leading to the kitchen and, found it also closed and the door inside that but the kitchen door itself was open. On entering the kitchen I looked at the fireplace and saw that the fire was not lighted for some days. I then entered the rooms in succession, found the beds empty just as they left them in the early morning. I did not take time to search further, for I only too well knew something serious had occurred. I darted out and made for the landing. When I reached there I informed Macormick that the place was deserted. He with some of the men came up a second time, so as to make sure, but unfortunately the first impression was only too true. William Macormick and myself proceeded to the lightroom where everything was in proper order. The lamp was cleaned. The fountain full. Blinds on the windows etc... We left and proceeded to board the steamer. On arrival Captain Harvie ordered me back again to the island, accompanied by Mr Macdonald (Buoymaster) A Campbell and A Lamont who were to do duty with me till timely aid should arrive.

We went ashore and proceeded up to the lightroom and lighted the light in the proper time that night and every night since. The following day we traversed the Island from end-to-end but still nothing to be seen to convince us how it happened. Nothing appears touched at East landing to show that they were taken from there. Ropes are all in their respective places, in the shelter just as they were left after the relief on the 7th. On the West side it is somewhat different. We had an old box halfway up the railway for holding the West landing mooring ropes and tackle, and it has gone. Some of the ropes it appears, got washed out of it, they lie strewn on the rocks near the crane. The crane itself is safe. The iron railings along the passage connecting railway with footpath to landing have started from their foundations and broken in several places, also railing around crane and handrail for making fast for boat is entirely carried away. Now there is nothing to give us an indication that it was there the poor men lost their lives, only that William Marshall has his seaboots on and oilskins, also Mr Ducat has his seaboots on. He had no oilskins, only an old waterproof coat and that is away. Donald Macarthur has his wearing coat left behind him, which shows as far as I know that he went out in shirt sleeves. He never used any other coat on previous occasions only the one I am referring to.

From the monthly return it is evident they are making notes to the 16th. Up to the 13th is marked in the book and 14th is marked on the slate, along with part of the fifteenth. On the 14th the prevailing state of the weather was westerly. Fifteenth the hour of extinguishing was noted on slate... I know that William Marshall never wore seaboots or oilskins, only when in connection with landings.

Your obedient servant, Joseph Moore

*

Joe took the path towards the west landing and veered off before he reached the steps for the small building he'd previously described to his comrades as the Teampull; the monks' cells and the tiny chapel. His rational mind said he was imagining all kinds of nonsense, but intuition told him he was right to take heed of the old stories – stories that told how the wrath of God would be brought to bear on those that paid scant attention to the sacred traditions.

Although he'd slept little on the previous night Joe had closed his eyes long enough to dream that he'd seen a monk beckoning to him. When he woke he felt sick to his stomach but nevertheless felt a great desire to commune with this monk's spirit. He'd never thought of himself as having particularly strong religious beliefs, but he considered that perhaps it might just clarify things for him. In his brief dream the monk had mysteriously borne him down to the sea to wash his sins away, but when he turned he had assumed the face of the poor dead Principal Lighthouse Keeper, James Ducat. Joe had screamed and screamed, and yet not screamed at all, in that terrible confusion that comes over those who sleep so deeply that dreams seem as real as the waking world.

By the time he left the lighthouse that morning the weather had brightened and he didn't really need his oilskins at all. He held his stone close in his pocket as he walked. The grass was springy and shone with morning dew. The Teampull stood grey and unchanging; the weathered stones blessed with lichen. The sun filtered weakly through the drifting clouds and the sea lay still on the horizon; no hint of storms, no threat of rain; just a cold breeze and a suggestion of ozone.

Joe stripped his clothes off behind the wall. He'd read about this ceremony. It was necessary for him to be naked. He knew it seemed like a strange thing to do. He knew his companions would think he was mad, but he also thought that re-enacting this age-old ceremony would go a long way to appeasing the spirits. He had deliberately slipped out of the lighthouse when the man on watch was busy. He'd taken great care not to wake the others. He'd dressed as if he was going down to the landing stage, just in case he was stopped on the way. In the lee of the Teampull no one from the kitchen could see him. No one would be able to guess his motives. He thought he would be safe from prying eyes. He could do what had to be done and be back inside before anyone knew any different.

God, but it was cold with nothing on. His pale skin came up in goosebumps. I am a wild man, he thought. May God take me and do what he will with me.

The grass gave beneath his feet as he walked sunwise round the old ruin. This was a 'deisal' turn. He felt very exposed but he counted three circuits, breathing low and long, taking care to focus on the task in hand and not let his mind wander to the ridiculous situation he had placed himself in. Coming to a standstill at the entrance he genuflected and then dropped to his knees and crawled into the small space. Then shivering, he knelt down in the grass. It was longer here inside the building and he was vaguely aware of its dampness and the smell of the earth. What he noticed most of all though was his own shame, which took him by surprise. That it had come to this; that it had come to cowering naked in a ruin in order to make peace with some unearthly and possibly devilish spirit of the isles. He closed his eyes and tried to conjure up the monk's spirit but nothing came to him save the ever-present wind, the caw of gulls and the baby cries of the seals. Even so these sounds were quieter. It was more peaceful here and Joe relaxed slightly. No one could see him. He could afford to explore the new sensations that came with this experience. He sat back on his haunches, feeling like a wild man. At one and the same time an intense sense of well-being and tranquillity washed over him. Yes, he was safe. Here in this sacred bone-cold place he was safe. It had been a long time since he'd felt like this. Fatigue took him and he slept; the first sound and dreamless sleep he'd had since landing on the island.

When he woke he couldn't tell how long he'd lain there, but his hands were frozen into claws, the nails digging softly into his palms causing tiny red marks like stigmata. Slowly he crawled backwards out of the Teampull, hoping on hope that no one had been spying on him.

They must not find me like this. They must not know. They must never know – and he meant the three sailors who were billeted with him although perhaps he was thinking, too, of the monk, or the dead lighthouse keepers. He only knew that whoever 'they' were, 'they' might already know about the madness that had taken hold of him. He was a marked man.

Gathering his clothes quickly, he pulled on trousers and jacket and bundled the rest under his coat as he stumbled forward. Could he slip back inside as easily as he'd slipped out? Or was there any point at all in bothering to hide his madness?

Leith 29th December 1900

Thomas Holman, Master of SS Archtor, *London 2193 tonnes states as follows:*

On the 15th inst. noon. The ships position by sights was 58 degrees 29 north, 11 degrees 36 west. About 120 miles west by north true from Flannan Islands.

We steered south east by east half speed until 4.00am of the 16th inst. Presumably passing within five miles of the north west of the Flannan Isles. We should have sighted the light at midnight on the 15th inst. Weather clear but strong, south-westerly wind with very heavy sea. At 7.00am 16th inst. we made the Butt of Lewis bearing east by south. The magnetic distance 16 miles, thus proving that we passed within six miles of the Flannans. The weather was clear and we should have seen the light easily, but notwithstanding a good look out saw nothing of the light in the islands, which we were trying to make as landfall after a very heavy passage with few sights across the Atlantic. Philadelphia to Leith.

I have heard the above statement read over and declare it correct.

NINE

$\mathcal{I}$t was an old building, the stones weathered and grey. The remnants of harness, bits of metal and the wheel from a cart littered the approach. The huge black doors stood open, and a reddish glow and the sound of hammering came from inside. Resting against the far door was a muddy bicycle. It looked sturdy enough, but it was hard to tell exactly under all that mud. Cal eyed the bicycle eagerly.

He'd had no joy finding transport across the island. Since arriving here he'd been given short shrift by everyone he met. He'd found an unheated room in a tiny hotel in the backstreets of the town and begun his enquiries there with the landlord, a man by the name of Macneill. At first Macneill thought Cal wanted directions to the Butt of Lewis Lighthouse and described in a long-winded way how he could hitch a lift with the mail cart and possibly old man Mcinnes, but not to rely on him because his sight was failing and he might fall off the road into a peat bog somewhere. Cal finally got it through to the hotel owner that he wanted the Flannans.

Macneill had looked him in the eye and in a very deliberate way said: 'That's in the middle of the Atlantic Ocean. You'll no find anyone who'll want to take you there.'

'I'll pay. There must be someone.'

Macneill sucked in his breath and shook his head.

'I cannae say. You could get a boat from Stornoway but you'd be better off abandoning the idea. There's been some rum goings on happening out there o late.'

'What kind of goings on?'

'Have you no seen the paper?'

Cal shook his head. He hadn't set sight on a news-paper since leaving Edinburgh and even there he hadn't been impressed.

'Here. I've a copy somewhere. Fresh in.'

Macneill disappeared. When he came back he was clutching a copy of the *Highland News*.

'There,' he said. 'Of course we knew about it already. Word travels fast. You'll be one of those journalist fellows too no doubt?'

Cal nodded. He was already scanning each page, looking for mention of the Flannans.

'I can't find anything.'

'Och well now, you'll be looking in the wrong place.'

'No… wait…' Yes, he'd found it.

Saturday, 29th December 1900

Disaster at Flannan Islands Lighthouse – Three men drowned.

A telegram was received on Thursday by Superintendent Smith of the Stornoway police from the west end of the Island of Lewis, conveying the sad intelligence of the loss on Friday or Saturday last of the three keepers of the Flannan Isles Lighthouse. No particulars have come to hand as to how the disaster occurred. The name of the keepers on duty were James Ducat (43), Thomas Marshall (28), and Donald Macarthur (40). The Lighthouse steamer proceeded during Thursday to the Flannan Isles but was unable to effect a landing due to the state of the sea surrounding the isles on which the lighthouse is built. Signals were exhibited from the steamer but no response came from the lighthouse, nor could any sign of human life be seen about the place. The tower appears to be intact but the lantern has not been lit from the past six nights. Great anxiety prevails concerning the men and conjecture is busy with all sorts of stories regarding their fate. The homes of the men are at Braescleit on Loch Roag, where a pier has also been built for the relieving steamer.

*

There it was – the men's homes were at Braescleit on Loch Roag. So he didn't necessarily have to go out to the Flannans. It might be that there would be someone at Braescleit who could give him the story he'd been looking for.

'Can I keep this?' he asked Macneill, not quite believing his luck. The blessed light had been out after all and this was a real life disaster. Okay, it had already hit the local news, but well, how far did the *Highland News* travel exactly? Certainly not as far as Philadelphia. In all likelihood no one at all save these Scottish peasants knew about this. But my, oh my, what a scoop. Cal could barely contain himself.

Excited, he shook the paper at Macneill.

'Well, can I have it or not?'

'Och now, it's the only one I've got…'

Cal was already folding the paper carefully. These were precious words containing some truth and also, Cal knew, some lies. In fact until he'd seen for himself it could all be lies. Yes, best think of it like that. Wouldn't do to go giving credit to what he knew would be a fine piece of reporting on his part to a foreign newspaper. No, this was source material and it must be preserved but it may not yet be true. Still, it felt a tiny bit uncanny, to have already been on the track of the missing light and suddenly to be apprised of a disaster. Fortuitous, Cal thought. Fortuitous indeed.

'Put it on my bill.'

Macneill considered.

'You were thinking of stopping then?'

'Maybe. Where can I find this Superintendent… what's his name?'

'Smith.'

'Yes, Smith. Where can I find him?'

Macneill shrugged.

'What d'you want him for?'

'Well, he'd be the first person told about this disaster, wouldn't he?'

'Maybe.'

'Then he'll be able to direct me to the widows of the poor souls lost from the lighthouse. If they're lost at all that is.'

'What d'you mean if they're lost at all?'

'All kinds of stories appear in the news. People like a good disaster. They like to hear about others' suffering.'

'No. No one around here like that. You'll no get anyone to say anything bad about the lighthouse men.'

'That's as maybe. But what about their wives? I'll bet they've got a thing or two to say. What if these keepers haven't been drowned? What if they've run off to sea? What if they've been captured by an enemy vessel?'

'What enemy?'

Cal shook his head. He was winding Macneill up deliberately to see what he could get out of him.

He said: 'Ah well, you can't tell what might really have happened to them.'

'You mean a sea serpent could o taken them?'

'You tell me.'

'No. I dinnae believe it.'

'Stranger things have happened.'

'No.'

Cal stuffed the paper into his overcoat pocket.

'Superintendent Smith? Where exactly would I find him?'

'The police station.' Macneill said 'po-leece'.

Cal waved goodbye on his way through the door.

Macneill shouted after him: 'Will you be wanting a bite to eat later?' But Cal was already out of earshot.

Macneill sniffed and mumbled: 'Because if you do then you'll be out o luck, you muckraker you. Feeding off peoples' grief.'

A while later Cal wandered into the police station and asked for Superintendent Smith.

'And who would be wanting him?' asked the Sergeant at the desk eyeing Cal with suspicion.

'Callum Robinson Esquire, of the *Philadelphia Star* newspaper.'

'A newspaperman, eh? And an American one at that if I'm not mistaken. What would an American newspaperman be wanting with us poor Lewis folks then?'

'Is Superintendent Smith here or not?'

'No, he is not.' The policeman sniffed. 'He's detained on important business.'

'When will he be back?'

'That would be telling now, wouldn't it?'

Cal frowned.

The Sergeant said: 'If there's nothing else…'

Cal thought for a moment. 'What do you know about the Flannan lighthouse?'

'Och now, there's a thing.'

Really they talked in riddles – a whole country of tall tale tellers.

'It's in the paper.'

'What paper would that be then?'

'The *Highland News*.' Cal flourished it at the police officer.

'Aye, that's a paper alright.'

'So what do you know about it?'

'I cannae talk about it,' and he tapped the side of his nose conspiratorially.

'Look,' Cal said, his patience sorely tested. 'All I want is some simple information about the report in the paper. It claims that a telegram was sent through to your Superintendent Smith here at the Stornoway police conveying "sad intelligence".'

'Aye, sad indeed.'

'And so did it?'

'Did it what?'

'Did the telegram come through to the police station here?'

'I cannae say.'

Cal exploded. 'What is it with you people? Why can't a single one of you give me a straight answer to a simple question?'

The Sergeant shrugged.

Cal shook his head. A couple of weeks earlier he might have really lost his temper. As it was he just felt defeated. Ace reporter? Who was he kidding? He slammed the door on his exit. It was all the anger he could muster. Outside his brief temper cooled quickly in the ice-sharp air. He could kill for a drink, but he decided against it. He needed to keep his wits about him if he was going to chase this story to its conclusion.

So when he came across the bicycle as he was walking back to the hotel the decision to steal it came on the spur of the moment. He didn't think he could face any more obstructive islanders. A bicycle would set him free. He'd ridden one when he was a child. It was easy. Macneill at the hotel had told him it was only fifteen miles to the west coast. Fifteen miles was nothing. Fifteen miles on a bicycle. Cal could do it. He knew he could.

He peeped into the smithy. A horse stamped and blew hot sweet air at the blacksmith who was leaning softly against the animal's bulk, lifting a hoof to inspect it. Cal waited and when the moment was right crossed the open door and laid claim to the bicycle by slipping into its saddle and pedalling away as fast as he could. He got a hundred yards up the road before he heard the blacksmith thundering after him. In his panic he lost the pedals and they spun round whacking him on the shins. This set up a wobble that he couldn't control. With the blacksmith gaining on him Cal careened up the kerb into a narrow alley between some houses. He scraped the wall and went over the handlebars. Luckily the bicycle was now blocking the path of the irate blacksmith, who was huffing and puffing, and cursing in Gaelic. Cal picked himself up and ran straight into a man loading sacks into a cart. Grabbing the carter by the arm, he shouted at him.

'Quick, hide me.'

The carter didn't seem to understand so Cal took the initiative and jumped into the back of the cart, covering himself with an empty sack.

'Go, please, go.'

By now the blacksmith had reached the end of the alley and had picked the bicycle up. He glanced down the road, but appeared not to notice Cal cowering in the back of the cart.

Cal waited to be discovered, but it never happened. The carter grunted, got up on the cart and urged his nag into action. The old horse lurched forward, the cart jolted and Cal heaved a sigh of relief.

A few yards on and the carter suddenly recovered powers of speech and grunted at his human cargo.

'It'll cost you.'

Cal responded with: 'Anything, just get me out of here.'

For once Cal's luck was in. The carter was travelling to Uig. He would be going as far as the junction at Garynahine. There Cal would be able to walk the last few miles to Braescleit. At least that was what Cal thought the carter meant. It was hard to tell exactly because English wasn't the carter's first language, but somehow Cal got the gist of it. He settled down for what turned out to be an uncomfortable ride over a largely unmade road.

The only signs of habitation in this great wet wilderness were a few scruffy black houses at Achmore, about halfway across the island. The carter said little, mostly because his English didn't stretch much beyond grunts after all. Rain misted the air and seeped inexorably through Cal's clothes. The gloom that he'd travelled with since leaving America, and which had steadily worsened now descended into feelings of desolation. Whereas he had arrived in a somewhat manic mood, and had been able to disregard the worst of the snubs he'd received from the locals, this silent journey across the interior of Lewis had forced him to confront a jumble of emotions he normally repressed rather successfully. The carter faced the weather with a stoicism that his passenger found hard to muster. Cal pulled his coat collar up and scowled. Needles of rain drove into his face, making it hard to focus on anything much but his raging inner demons. He ignored the scenery and so couldn't appreciate that on a clear day the Isle of Lewis would be a beautiful place.

Seven miles and what seemed like several hours further on they reached the Garynahine junction. Cal had travelled to the end of the world. There had been only a few scattered ruins since the houses at Achmore and these he hadn't paid much attention to, so when the big slated building at the junction loomed ahead, and the carter called his horse to a halt, Cal thought that this must be a way-station on the road to hell. The carter mumbled something and indicated towards the barn of a place in the distance. As awful as the journey had been, and as wet as he was, Cal was loath to leave the relative safety of the cart for the rutted track that would lead him away on foot. Looking back along the road Cal noticed another, closer house than the big building the carter was indicating. Cal shook his head.

'No, not there. There,' and he pointed to the house behind them.

'No, no,' the carter said, and he turned on his seat and made to shove Cal out.

'Here, watch out,' Cal shouted. 'What's the matter with you?'

'No there. That's the doctor. There. That's the hotel.'

If that was a hotel then it was shut up for the season. The path up to it was quagmire and no lights showed in the windows. Cal nodded disconsolately, unable to muster the strength to argue further. Muttering profanities, he slipped down from the cart and stood there in a puddle surveying the route to the so-called hotel. If the house belonged to the local doctor then it was surely the better option. A doctor wouldn't turn him away, would he? Not in the state he had arrived in. Choosing to ignore the carter's recommendation Cal squelched through the puddles to what he thought was surely the doctor's house.

A woman answered the door. She listened carefully as Cal introduced himself, but didn't actually appear to understand anything he said. She just cocked her head on one side, opened the door a few inches more so that she could see the hotel better, and pointed towards it.

'Garynahine,' she said slowly. Cal sighed. Not the doctor's then. There really was no point in trying to argue with these people.

*

The swollen sea heaved, threatening to upturn the *Hesperus*, but she made the east landing on Flannan all the same. Superintendent Robert Muirhead, lighthouse keepers John Milne and Donald Jack duly disembarked, the keepers to take over from the hard-pressed sailors who had remained on the isle, Muirhead to investigate the disaster. Captain Harvie agreed to wait for a signal from Muirhead to take him back to the shore station, together with the sailors Macdonald, Campbell, and Lamont.

Joe was filling in the log when Muirhead stamped through the kitchen door, the two new keepers in his wake. They shook hands, Muirhead giving Joe a look of deepest sadness. The other keepers simply nodded their heads briefly. There was nothing they could say to make things easier. Joe filled the kettle to brew a pot of tea. Archie hovered in the background and when the moment was right showed the new men to their billets.

Preliminaries over, Muirhead cupped his drink in his hands and gazed long into the fire before speaking.

'My guess is you don't want to talk about it.'

Joe barely nodded.

'But you know that in the long run it will be better for everyone if you do.'

Again, barely a nod.

'Tell me about when you landed. What you found… or didn't.' Muirhead carefully placed his cup on the floor by his chair and leaned forwards a little.

Joe eyed him nervously. Of course he knew this man. He'd met him several times before. Never in these kind of circumstances though. Never to explain about the death of another. He looked up at the Superintendent, felt tears well in his eyes and immediately blinked them away and stared into the middle distance.

'We sounded the whistle and fired a rocket but they didn't hear us. That was the first thing I suppose.'

'Go on.'

'I thought they were here somewhere. I thought at first they were taken ill in their beds, but they weren't. And then there was the chair.'

'The chair?'

'Upturned. Like someone had got up suddenly.' Joe paused, gathering his thoughts, which were jumbled with all kinds of inconsequentialities he couldn't understand.

'I wondered why they'd left it like that, but of course they weren't here, were they? They weren't here.'

Muirhead nodded in agreement.

'We looked everywhere but we couldn't find them.'

'We?'

'Me and the Second Mate, William Macormick. He came ashore with me the second time. Archie too come to think of it.'

'So you made two trips from *Hesperus*?'

'Yes. I came the first time and then Mac came the second time to check with me.'

Muirhead considered. 'When you came the first time. Apart from the chair what did you notice?'

'The quiet. There had been a terrible storm. It had died a bit but it was still fearsome windy, and yet it was so quiet in here.' Joe listened for a moment as it trying to conjure those moments. All he could hear now was the crackle of the fire, the slow steady tick of the clock, the faint voices of his colleagues in the background, and the gentle hiss of his own breath warming the air as he exhaled. He stared at the fire until the heat hurt his eyes and he had to look away and blink.

'Not like now,' he said. 'There's a noise now that wasn't here before.' He knew he sounded mad. If that were so then Muirhead would have no option but to recommend his dismissal. Perhaps that's what he hoped for. He didn't really know. He just knew he didn't want to be here.

The fire spat a coal out onto the rug. The Superintendent stamped the ember aside quickly.

'Go on.'

Joe drew a long breath.

'When we couldn't find them we went back to the tender and told Captain Harvie. He said I had to stay and man the light. I would have done that anyway, I would. I didn't need to be told.'

'You know your duty, lad.'

'Aye, I know my duty, but that doesnae make it easy to carry out.'

'No, I don't suppose it does.'

'I don't want to be here. There's too many reminders. It's too much to ask of me, even though I know it's my duty. I don't want to let the Northern Lighthouse Board down, I don't, but I can't stay here.' Joe wanted to ask for a transfer but he hadn't expected to ask like this. He'd expected to be a little more circumspect in his request.

'That's something I will have to consider.'

'I didn't mean I wouldn't stay…'

'I understand.'

Joe wasn't sure that Muirhead did.

He ventured: 'I've seen things.'

The older man's interest perked up.

'What kind of things?'

'Maybe not seen exactly. Felt more like.' Slow down, Joe thought. Best not let on too much.

'Yes?'

Joe glanced at Muirhead, trying to gauge if he trusted him enough to tell him about the forerunners. He decided no. He didn't want the Superintendent thinking he was going mad. No, that wouldn't do at all.

'No, it's of no consequence.'

Muirhead shrugged.

'When the time is right, laddie. When the time is right… You searched the landings of course?'

'The next day. We couldn't land at the west landing because of the tide and the swell. There'd been a storm raging for days. It was what had caused our delay out here. Well, when I went down to the west landing that following day the sea was still fierce.' He paused for a moment, remembering the baby cries of the seals.

'The crane platform was fine. Nothing out of order at all. But it was strange because the ropes were strewn over the rocks and the box they are usually kept in was upturned. There were other ropes though that were coiled as usual. I'd best show you. I haven't moved anything.'

'Very wise I'm sure. What else can you remember?'

'It's odd that only two oilskins are missing,' and here Joe glanced at the pegs where the oilskins hung.

'Only two you say?'

'Mr Ducat must have been wearing his boots and oilskin. Tommie was wearing his, but Donald left his on the peg.'

'And you only wear waterproofs when you're going down to the landings.'

Joe remembered his sojourn to the Teampull wearing his own oilskins.

'Yes,' he said, feeling guilty.

'And so they meant to go down to the landings and something happened that caused the third man, Donald Macarthur, to go out without his waterproofs.'

'I suppose.'

Muirhead stood up and looked out of the window.

'From here you can't see the west landing.'

'You can see the track.'

'And Donald Macarthur was inside while they were out?'

'Aye, seems likely.'

'Can you see the west landing from the gallery?'

'No, not properly. The tip of the crane maybe, but no not even that.'

'So if something happened to the other two how would he know?'

'He wouldn't unless he went out there to check.'

'In which case he would wear his oilskins.'

Joe nodded morosely. It didn't make sense.

'I believe an experiment is in order.' Muirhead turned back to Joe and smiled gently. 'Come, laddie. You go down to the west landing and I'll see if I can spy you. Go to both the crane platform and the landing itself if you can reach it. I'll watch from here and I'll send one of the other lads aloft to see if you can be spied from the gallery.'

'If you think it will help.'

'I do, laddie, I do.'

Joe grabbed his oilskins.

He was pleased that Muirhead was here. Even though the other men were strong enough in mind and body, Muirhead was a solid presence that represented the authority of the Northern Lighthouse Board. He travelled the Highlands and Islands throughout the year, visiting lighthouses in every location. He must have come across some fantastic tales in his time, heard stories that would make your hair stand on end. Joe walked the little rail track to its end above the west landing and realised that he felt safer with Muirhead here, as if nothing could touch him.

Casting a look back to the lighthouse, he could see that from this point above the west landing the kitchen windows were still visible but that just a little further down they would be out of sight. My, but it was cold this morning. The wind whipped the crests of the breaking waves to foam, and away out into the Atlantic the sea appeared choppy.

Here it was then, the crane platform, just as he'd left it the first time he'd inspected it a few days earlier, the ropes and the upturned box. He looked back again at the lighthouse. The kitchen building had disappeared from view now; only the tower was visible. He walked down a few more steps, taking them slowly, aware again of the twisted railings and wondering once more at the force of the waves to torture the metal thus. Unlike the previous occasion though he felt more comfortable. No bad memories. No strange premonitions. Maybe the ceremony had worked. Maybe he'd appeased whatever strange force existed here on Eilean Mor.

Able to think more rationally, he tried to work out what could have actually happened to the men. He couldn't be sure of course that they had been at the west landing when the tragedy had happened, but it seemed more likely than the east. Sheltered from the worst of the Atlantic weather the eastern landing was always calmer and there were fewer cross currents. By comparison the west landing faced the brunt of each storm rolling across the vast motioned ocean from the Grand Banks way out on the eastern shores of the Americas. Interestingly, here at the west landing the inlet was very narrow so that even when the sea was relatively calm the waves channelled in and upwards. Skiopageio – that was what the end of the inlet was called. On a stormy day the sea boomed hollow in this rocky funnel. He'd heard it himself – even watched the waves pounding upward. It had never crossed his mind that they might contain enough force to carry a man off. Of course he should have realised. He'd been at sea often enough in a storm to know that a rogue wave could catch you unawares if you weren't keeping watch. But these men were seasoned keepers. They had more sense than to deliberately put themselves in danger. Something must have happened to take their mind off the business at hand. Something supernatural perhaps?

Oh God, he was back to that.

He mustn't think about it. There was a rational explanation. There had to be. If they had come down to the west landing and got into trouble somehow, no matter what had happened, how would Donald Macarthur, doing the washing up in the lighthouse kitchen know unless he could see them? Joe squinted up the steps. The Superintendent was coming towards him. He waved Joe to come up.

'I cannae see you from the kitchen. Not when you're down there, or here on the platform,' he said when Joe reached him.

'I knew as much,' Joe replied.

'Look here. The crane's jib has been lowered and secured.'

Joe nodded.

'And they had time to lash the canvas covering and the wire rope. So all here is in order.'

'Did you see the ropes higher up?' Joe asked.

'The mooring ropes and such like?'

'Aye.'

'I did, and I think they give us an idea of what may have happened here.'

'How come?'

'Let us consider that Principal Keeper Ducat and Tommie Marshall came down here to secure the crane and landing equipment.'

'Why here though? Anything could have happened and it didn't have to have happened here.' Joe shuddered. He meant something other than natural, but he couldn't tell the Superintendent. Not just yet anyway.

Muirhead considered for a moment.

'I thought that, but the west always comes worst off in a storm. The leeward shore, laddie. The leeward shore. And the crane's here. They'd want to make sure everything was fast. The sea is running high today, but during a storm it would be almost impossible to stand here without suffering the consequences. I would say you cannae get down to the landing stage even today.'

'No.'

'Then think what it would have been like. You've been here when the weather is bad.'

'Aye, that's true.' And it was. Joe had been down to the crane platform himself during a storm to do the exact same thing the men must have done on that fateful day. He tried to remember what he'd felt at those times – not the danger inherent in the situation. That didn't really come into it when he was busy. Usually that only happened if he thought about it later. And of course lately he'd let his fears get the better of him. When the weather was really bad there was no point in going out at all save that the equipment had to be maintained at all times. Even so the lighthouse had only been up and running for a year. In that time they had encountered all kinds of weather conditions and seas. Today for instance, the horizon was shrouded in grey and although the sea was choppy, in the far distance it heaved in a slower, more determined way.

'I've never seen the waves so high as to carry a man off,' Joe commented. No, that wasn't correct. For all that they must maintain the equipment there were times when they wouldn't even consider stepping outside. All the equipment in the world was useless if there were no men to tend the light. No, they would not place themselves in danger when the sea was running high. They just wouldn't.

Muirhead went up the steps a little way and bent to examine a large block of stone.

'Look here. This slab has been dislodged.'

Joe frowned.

The Superintendent pointed back up to the end of the track.

'It comes from up there. It's been carried all the way down the path and deposited here at the top of the steps.'

'How do you know?'

'Can you no see where it sat in the groove there?'

Joe squinted. No he couldn't. He wished he'd noticed more and felt less when he'd made his first reconnoitre. Perhaps there were more signs he'd missed. Perhaps Muirhead would think him incompetent and have him dismissed.

'I'd like a transfer,' Joe said suddenly, stopping on his ascent of the steps.

'Well now, where's that come from?' Muirhead turned to eye the young keeper.

'I don't think I can carry on here under the circumstances.'

'I'll take it under consideration.' Muirhead nodded. 'Yes, it may be better if you were moved, but not just yet, eh laddie? Not just yet. We've work to do. Look.' He pointed. 'The lifebuoy has disappeared completely.'

It was true. There was supposed to be a lifebuoy lashed to the railings. All that remained was the rope by which it had been fastened.

'I cannae believe they both got into trouble at the same time,' Joe remarked, his mind flitting from one thought to another. 'One of them perhaps, and the other tried to rescue him.'

'We can't be sure of that.'

'We can't be sure of anything.' Joe was warming slightly to this. It was more positive than worrying about holy men or ghostly forerunners. Those thoughts still bothered him of course, but he knew that if he could just keep his mind on more earthly matters he might be alright.

'And if you cannae see the men from the window then surely Donald wouldn't have known that anything was amiss until they didn't come back?'

'Ah, you've hit the nail on the head, laddie. The Occasional would have put his own oilskins on to go out and look. And he didn't.'

'So it happened quickly you mean? Before he had a chance to think about it?'

'Yes,' Muirhead started to lead the way back to the lighthouse.

'But what then? If he couldn't see what was happening?'

'We're back to something happening to one of the men first and the other running for help.'

'And Donald would have seen whichever one it was coming up the track and run straight out.' Yes, that made sense.

'Sir, what about the transfer?'

'I don't know, laddie. Like I said, I'll think about it.'

At the top of the ridge the two men stopped, the onshore wind ruffling Joe's hair. In front of them the lighthouse stood firm, testament to the engineering skills of the Stevensons.

'They could have been blown out to sea of course,' he conjectured. At times the wind was strong enough.

'Unlikely,' replied Muirhead. 'The wind was westerly. No, I'm pretty certain they were washed away. Either both together or one after the other. I favour the second.'

'It would have to be an unusually large wave to do that.'

'One of them – and we can't be sure which one of course – one of them was caught off balance by a huge wave and washed away. The other perhaps may not have known what happened for a minute or two. Or maybe he watched and was helpless to do anything. When he realised he couldn't rescue his colleague he would have dashed up the steps to fetch help.

'Up in the lighthouse the Occasional would be completely unaware of the trouble his fellow lighthouse keepers were in. He may have seen the survivor waving and shouting to him as he ran back. He'd have run outside without thinking. If our survivor had got as far as the lighthouse itself Mr Macarthur would have reached for his wet weather gear. So I think it likely that he just ran outside when he saw his colleague.'

Here Muirhead paused as if seeing the incident in his mind's eye.

'Mr Macarthur and the surviving man ran down to the crane platform together. Perhaps the stone block crashed down after them.'

Joe shuddered. With the wind blowing in their faces and the waves crashing round them the men would search in vain.

'Perhaps they took risks they wouldn't normally have considered,' Muirhead commented. 'Put yourself in their position. Tell me what you would do.'

Joe closed his eyes. Here they were at the water's edge, one man down. He may have been washed straight out to sea, but given the way the water ran into this inlet only to be sucked down and funnelled up, it was more likely that the man's body was visible from time to time in the tumultuous waters. Panic stricken they would try to rescue him even though they both knew he was dead. You didn't survive long in these waters even when they were calm. It was too cold and the hidden rocks too dangerous.

'If they were washed away together it wouldn't have been so bad,' Joe said. 'If one went before the other then the remaining man would have had a hard time of it unless he was washed away almost immediately afterwards. It would be a nightmare to be left the last man alive.' And the horror of what he'd just said struck him. What if the last man alive, and it seemed as if that was Donald Macarthur, what if he couldn't stand the strain of being left here alone? What if he'd thrown himself after his fellow keepers? What if he'd committed suicide?

Muirhead was nodding. 'Can you imagine trying to rescue two men on your own? Impossible.'

'They didn't know what hit them, did they? They were just taken by the sea and that's that.' And even though Joe had known all along that was what had happened to the men he'd lived and worked alongside, it was really only now that he admitted to himself the reality of the situation. No ghosts, no strange monks, no phantoms, just the sea and the relentless harvest of men's lives. Had he been able to he would right then have turned his back on the vast Atlantic, but it was no use. The great ocean was all around him. The sea appeared in his line of sight every which way he turned.

*

Cal presented himself at the door of the Garynahine Hotel in a terrible state. It was true that the premises were closed for the season, but it was also true that Mrs Mackenzie was a hospitable woman who wasn't about to turn a cold wet foreigner away in a hurry. Soaked through, Cal's skin had taken on a deathly pallor and he could barely speak without wheezing. The bitterness of the weather had taken root in his bones and had he been refused shelter he thought he would surely have died, if not from the cold then certainly from the misery that accompanied it. Mrs Mackenzie took one look at Cal and ushered him inside.

The hallway wasn't exactly warm but the parlour had a big fire that crackled in the grate. Cal dripped on a rug until Mrs Mackenzie relieved him of his topcoat and encouraged him to remove his waterlogged shoes. She provided slippers and a warm towel and left him to get warm while she went to find tea and a bite to eat for her guest.

Cal stared morosely into the flame and let the heat redden his face. The pain gave him some insight into how futile his journey to the western isles really was.

It's a whim, he thought. A premonition that had been based on nothing much but a missing light and the cussedness of officialdom that refuses to cooperate… and here I am in this bloody hellhole and a damned newspaper report turns up and proves me right. I knew something was going on. I just knew it. Look at me now – reduced to begging a bed for the night off some grinning peasant.

'What's that, dear?' Mrs Mackenzie had returned with the tea.

Cal looked up at her, unaware that he'd been thinking out loud.

'You get yourself nice and warm and then I'll show you to a room. We're not really open but I cannae turn a stranger away on a night like this now, can I?'

Cal scowled. He knew he should feel grateful, and some little part of him did, but he couldn't muster the strength to respond as he should.

Mrs Mackenzie didn't seem to notice. She was a friendly woman, well liked by the locals. She'd only recently married again after several years of running the hotel as a widow. Her new husband was one John Mackenzie and he was something of a charmer. But whereas Mrs Mackenzie treated all alike, Mr Mackenzie only turned on his charm for those of similar social standing to himself.

'You were lucky to come on the hotel, dearie. Most strangers go right down to the village and then find themselves directed back along the road. It can be difficult to escape the hospitality of the good folk around here. Doubtless you've noticed how they'll ask you inside and press a wee dram on you.'

'No,' Cal mumbled. No, he hadn't.

'Well now we're famous around here for our hospitality. Of course there's the hotel but we're a private establishment really. We don't cater for the riffraff.' She gave a little laugh.

Cal wasn't sure if she meant he fitted the description of 'riffraff' and had been taken in as a charity case, or if she had seen through his bedraggled state to the gentleman he felt himself to be.

As if she read his mind Mrs Mackenzie nodded and said: 'Of course I could tell you were a gent. A proper gent. I can see that straight away in a man. My husband, now he's a proper gent too. Won't stand for riffraff at all. I don't mind, me. We're all God's creatures, aren't we? Drink your tea, dear. That's right.'

Cal wished she'd shut up. All he wanted was a place to lay his head for a few hours.

'You said something about a room.'

It was the first time he'd really spoken a whole sentence since his arrival. Mrs Mackenzie caught his accent and smiled.

'Well now, what's an American gent doing on our fine island may I ask?'

Oh God this woman. Why couldn't she shut up?

'It's a long story.'

'Ah well, stories are something we've a lot of time for if you've a mind to tell it. But look at me now, keeping you from drying out.' She patted him on the shoulder. 'I'll leave you be for a while and get your room ready. When you're rested you can tell me and Mr Mackenzie both that long story.'

Cal smiled wanly. Bloody do-gooder, he thought and he buried his head in his hands. The story was lost – had to be under the circumstances. Why oh why had he ever come to this Godforsaken place?

*

Annabella was busy trying to peer through the tiny droplets of rain on the window that magnified the world outside. It was hard because they were so small and she had to look through several at once. She could see a strange fragmented landscape and in it someone coming up the road from the Breascleit pier. It was difficult to make out who it was exactly because the magnifying droplets scattered the image as if she was looking through broken glass. After struggling with this for a few moments she reluctantly wiped the window with her sleeve and Superintendent Robert Muirhead appeared in her line of sight.

'Mama,' she shouted. 'It's that man.' She jumped down from her perch in the parlour window seat and ran into the kitchen where her mother was busy with the baking. For all that had happened life went on much as it always had. There were still mouths to be fed: four children didn't feed themselves.

'Mama,' Annabella whined, 'it's that man from the Board.'

Mary set her bowl to one side and wiped her hands on her apron. Annabella stood blinking, wondering, waiting. Her mother had been strange these last few days – distant. The wee girl knew it was because of what had happened out at the lighthouse, but everyone was being so strange, so quiet around her, that she still couldn't really work out what it was that they were keeping quiet about.

Will Ross in particular had taken to staring out to sea, his eyes glazed over. Annabella could tell he had been crying, but he would never admit it and she dared not ask him directly. Of course Tommie wasn't coming home, she knew that much. Tommie was the one that was meant to be here now, but no one had come in his place – and for all her confusion somewhere in the back of her mind Annabella knew too that none of the lighthouse keepers would ever come home from the Flannan Isles. Not Tommie, not Mr Macarthur, and not her father. No, not him either, though he was still fresh in her mind. He'd spun her round in the front garden on his last farewell. He'd taken her up in his arms and kissed her on both cheeks. His moustache had tickled her. She bit her lip. Perhaps Joe would be lost too.

The knock on the front door made Mary jump even though Annabella's warning had alerted her to the Superintendent's arrival.

'Stay in here,' she said to Annabella.

'Why?'

'Because I say so.'

They always did that, the grown-ups – they excluded her from the important things in life. Annabella vowed never to be left out of anything again and boldly followed her mother into the hall.

Mary glanced in the mirror and patted her hair in place before opening the door.

Muirhead bowed his head and offered her his hand to shake.

'Ah Mr Muirhead, won't you come in?' Mary said, her voice quivering.

'Thank you kindly, my dear lady.'

Hat in hand Muirhead allowed Mary to show him into the parlour where he stood nervously eyeing the picture of Queen Victoria hanging over the mantelpiece.

'It's a terrible business, Mrs Ducat. There's no saying otherwise. Let me offer you my condolences and those of the Northern Lighthouse Board.'

Mary sat down suddenly, her skirt puffing up as she did so. Annabella rushed to her side, but Mary waved her away.

'Go and find your big sister. Tell her we've a guest and to bring tea and cakes.'

'No, really,' Muirhead said. 'Don't put yourself to too much trouble.'

'It's no trouble. We bake every day.' She looked blank and then repeated the phrase, 'every day.'

Annabella didn't move. She didn't want to go and find her sister. She knew if she did that she would miss some vital piece of information about what had happened to the three men, and she couldn't bear to think that they were talking about them behind her back. There had been too much of that already.

'Go,' her mother commanded.

Annabella stood her ground. Oh but Mama could stare so, yet here she was dissolving into tears. Reluctantly the little girl backed out of the room. Should she be crying too? Why was it that although she felt sad she couldn't cry? Outside in the hall she leant against the door and listened to her mother's soft tears. All this crying made her feel guilty. Papa wasn't coming back. Papa would never ever come back and yet she couldn't cry for him and she didn't understand why.

*

Joe lay in his bunk and for the first time since he landed on the island allowed himself to close his eyes without worrying what sleep might bring by way of dreams. He was so tired he slept deeply for several hours and when he woke it was quiet and dark. He judged it was about three in the morning. Usually he would have woken in a sweat but he felt strangely calm and lay for a while before slipping out of bed and ascending the stairs to the gallery. Donald Jack was up here too, but when he saw Joe he went down to make himself a cup of tea.

Joe edged round the gallery. It was hard to see out and he had to shade his eyes with his hands against the glass. The gentle whirr of the mechanism inside and the howl of the wind outside sealed him in a bubble of sound he had become so used to that he didn't usually give it much thought. But tonight, because he was more rested than he had been in a long time, he became aware of the emptiness of this sound, for although the combined noise had a resonance he recognised, it also contained an element of unreality. He wondered if it was just his state of mind. He felt rested, that was true, but with this newfound peace had come a heightened sense of the supernatural. Although he had been scared of almost everything he'd encountered so far on this relief his psychic ability was limited to that which his fertile mind allowed him to imagine. Now it told him that fear didn't have to exist side by side with the supernatural – that it was perfectly possible to hold the fear at bay and observe the phenomena, however that might present itself.

Joe peered into the darkness beyond the gallery. He could see now how his fears had blinded him to any and all possible truths. There was no reason why the explanation the Superintendent had come up with was any less truthful than the explanation that now seemed to present itself to Joe: that something otherworldly had happened here, and that the weather and the natural elements had conspired to hide this by taking the lighthouse keepers and offering in their stead ghostly phenomena. The more Joe pondered this the more it seemed to make perfect sense.

Donald Jack appeared at the top of the stairs.

'I've brought you a cup.'

Joe took the proffered cup gratefully.

'Can you hear that?' he asked, the steam curling its mist around his face as his sipped his tea.

The other keeper cocked his head to listen.

'What?'

'I don't know, but it's there.'

'The Super said you'd been spooked. He said to treat you with kid gloves.'

'He did, did he? Well maybe you should. Maybe you should.' Joe scowled. What had else had Muirhead said? That he was going mad? That he should be watched?

'He didnae mean anything by it. He wanted us to keep an eye on you.'

Joe gave the other man a sideways look.

Donald Jack went on: 'He was worried about you. Thought you'd been through enough and shouldn't have to go through anymore.'

'Why'd he leave me here then? Answer me that. I told him I wanted a transfer. I asked him. I said I couldn't stay here.'

'There's not the men to spare. Not with what happened and all.'

'That's not my fault.'

'No one's saying it is. It's just the way things are the now.' Jack set his cup down by his feet and ran his sleeve absentmindedly over one of the prisms to shine it. He kept his face turned away as he did so.

'You'll be out of here on the next relief.'

'I want away from here today.'

'That's no going to happen.'

Joe made to go down stairs. At the top he stopped and turned to Jack who had taken his place, back to the light, back to Joe.

'They'll come for me next, they will.'

'Who's that then?'

'If you havenae seen them then I cannae explain in words you'd understand.'

'Try me.'

Joe took a few steps down. 'I'm no afraid anymore. If they come, they come. I'm no afraid now.'

Donald Jack nodded. Joe knew instinctively that this meant the keeper hadn't a clue. He was just being polite; doing what had been asked of him. Joe wound his way to the bottom of the stairs. No, he wasn't afraid anymore. He still didn't like being there, but at least his fears had somehow been transformed into a kind of knowledge; a deep-seated feeling that as much as he didn't like what had happened it had somehow been inevitable, and therefore alright. Wasn't it true that knowledge was power? Did that mean that even if he couldn't exactly say what that knowledge was, even if it was more a 'knowing' deep inside, it still meant that he could handle the strange visions that presented themselves to him. It meant he didn't have to be scared out of his mind the whole time. He could function as a lighthouse keeper – do his job and yet still keep separate the part of him that had the "knowing". Yes, that was it. The 'knowing' was something special – a gift. And knowing the means of your own death, well that meant that he could prepare for it. He could make provision for those that loved him. His three colleagues hadn't died for naught. They may be beckoning him from beyond the grave but at least he knew now that his own demise would come swiftly and that his companions were waiting for him from beyond their watery grave. Joe slipped back into his bunk, his trusty stone gripped tight in his palm. Sleep found him quickly.

*

Archie Lamont leant forward in his chair. He had been sitting in the deep shadow by the window. He was a canny old fellow. He'd watched Joe get up. He heard the conversation up in the gallery, and he caught wind of Joe's change. Lamont leant back in his chair again. The lad needed watching and that was what he would do.

TEN

❦

Things were looking up for Cal. After a decent night's sleep he felt a little more like his old self. Mrs Mackenzie had managed to dry his clothes out and, as he slicked down his hair in the mirror, a young boy shouted through the door that he'd brought his boots, which had been scraped free from mud and polished up. Glancing outside he noticed that the rain had let up and that a weak sun was shining. The view showed him a pattern of green, fringed in the far distance with stone walls and a watery horizon where the land met the sea and the sea met the sky.

The smell of breakfast greeted him as he opened the door to retrieve his boots. He reckoned it was about half past ten. His pocket watch was waterlogged and had stopped the day before so he couldn't say for sure. A shout came up the stairs but he couldn't understand what was being said.

Cal tied his laces and pulled on his jacket. Sadly, his flask had disappeared but for the first time in quite a while he wasn't much bothered by its absence. All in all he thought it remarkable that he was in such good shape. He was actually looking forward to breakfast.

Mr John Mackenzie was sitting at the head of the table reading a newspaper when Mrs Mackenzie ushered Cal through the door and showed him a chair.

'Take no mind o Mr Mackenzie, my dear. He's just popped in for a wee while.' Mrs Mackenzie offered Cal a bowl and indicated that he should help himself to porridge and then to whatever else took his fancy from the food laid out on the sideboard. It was all very civilised.

A voice bellowed out from behind the newspaper.

'Mind and tell him we aren't open to riffraff.'

'Hush now, John. He's had a terrible time of it, haven't you, dear?'

Mrs Mackenzie tapped the table with a spoon.

'I'll thank you not to read at my breakfast table.'

Her husband shook the newspaper out and folded it. He looked over the top of his glasses at Cal and then took them off and slipped them in his top pocket.

'You'll be moving on soon I should think.'

'I was hoping to make this my centre of activity for the time being.'

'And what activity would that be now?' asked Mackenzie. 'My wife tells me you're a reporter. We don't get too many of them all the way out here.'

Cal stuffed himself hungrily. People usually reacted with animosity towards him once they knew what he did for a living, so he wasn't that bothered by the sarcasm in Mackenzie's voice.

'Tell me Mr….'

'Robinson,' Cal said through a mouthful of porridge.

'Mr Robinson.' Mackenzie sounded thoughtful now. 'Tell me what your activities are precisely that you will require the use of my establishment as your "centre". We are out of season right now. We don't cater for passers-by as a rule.'

'I wasn't passing by.'

'You weren't? Well then, pray tell what were you doing?'

Cal slurped his tea noisily.

'Investigating.'

'Investigating?'

'Hmm.'

John Mackenzie drummed his fingers on the table. Cal looked up and met his host's icy stare, but before he could explain exactly what he meant Mrs Mackenzie bustled back in.

'There's a Superintendent Muirhead in the public room from the Northern Lighthouse Board. Says do we know the whereabouts o your father.'

Mackenzie bellowed, 'No, I bloody don't know where he is.'

'Well now, that's no exactly the truth because we do know where he is, don't we? Perhaps you'd better come and talk to him because I have to attend to Mr Robinson here.'

Cal laid his spoon in the bowl and wiped his mouth with a napkin.

'There's no need,' he said. 'I'd like a word with him myself.'

Mackenzie pointed accusatorily at Cal and said: 'You're here about the men that disappeared. I know your sort. Pushing your nose into things where it's not wanted. Out. I want you out.'

'Now dear, do you think that's entirely wise? He's done no harm and he was terrible taken with the cold when he arrived. Besides it's Hogmanay tonight and we've a crowd coming,' Mrs Mackenzie fretted. 'I wouldn't want to turn Mr Robinson out on Hogmanay.'

John Mackenzie ignored her and instead made his way to the public room. Mrs Mackenzie trotted behind and Cal brought up the rear. He wasn't going to miss this for the world.

'Mr Mackenzie.' Superintendent Muirhead offered his hand. Mr Mackenzie shook it and the two men took up seats opposite each other. Cal noticed how Mackenzie nodded to his wife as if to dismiss her, but she clearly wasn't going to play the good little woman and sat at a small table behind her husband. Cal hung back in the doorway. He'd already worked out how Mackenzie's mind worked – one rule for the upper class and one for the lower. He knew that the proprietor of the Garynahine Hotel had pegged him as being from the latter and obviously this man Muirhead's status, as an official from the illustrious Northern Lighthouse Board, meant he was one of the former. Cal smiled to himself. Animosity always made for a good story.

Mackenzie threw a worried glance over his shoulder towards his wife, but she sat quite calmly, her hands clasped in her lap. It was quite clear where the balance of power really lay.

'Sir, I was directed to your establishment by the good folk at the Shore Station.'

Mrs Mackenzie nodded. 'Taigh Mòr they call it.'

'Yes,' Muirhead agreed. 'The big house.'

Cal slipped a notebook out from his inside pocket. He could learn a lot just by hanging back and listening.

'What is it you want with us?' Mackenzie asked.

'I was given to understand you might know the where-abouts of your father, Roderick Mackenzie.'

'No, cannae say's I do.' Mackenzie glanced at his wife again.

'You know perfectly well, John, that like as no he'll be at Mevaig.'

'Aye, I suppose.'

'Mevaig.' Muirhead licked a pencil and wrote the name down in a black notebook.

'What would you be wanting wi my father now?' Mackenzie asked.

'Ah well. He was trusted with the lookout's post.'

'Aye, that he was.'

'And I need to ask him a few questions relevant to the terrible loss of the lighthouse men.'

Cal's ears perked up. This was more like it.

Mrs Mackenzie shook her head sadly. 'Terrible business. Terrible.'

Cal waited for more, but the others had fallen silent. The clock ticked ominously in the hall. Cal shuddered as if someone had just walked over his grave.

It was Mrs Mackenzie who broke the silence. 'Be careful and ask for the right place mind or you'll be taken on a merry dance. Ask for the gamekeeper.'

She paused, considering. 'Mind you now he may just as well be at the croft at Aird Uig.'

'Which would it be now?' Muirhead cocked his head.

'I'd try Mevaig. Mind, Gallon Head now, that's where you're really wanting to go, isn't it?'

Muirhead smiled. 'The lookout. Aye. That's where I'd like to go. But it's vital I speak with Roderick Mackenzie as soon as possible, and if he's no there…'

Mackenzie snorted. 'You'll no get there by road that's for sure. There is no road. Boat'll be your best bet. Aye, a boat.'

'From Calanais, or Breascleit,' offered Mrs Mackenzie. 'The tender perhaps? It could take you what, John? Two or three hours. Yes. Two or three hours of your time.'

'Then I must away,' mused Muirhead. 'I shouldnae waste any more of your good time. I'll make haste now. You've been most kind. Most helpful.' He rose and offered his hand to John Mackenzie again. 'Thank you sir, for your hospitality. I have a long journey ahead of me and I won't keep you a moment longer than necessary.'

Mackenzie frowned but shook hands nevertheless. Mrs Mackenzie followed the Superintendent.

'You've a cart waiting for you outside?'

'Aye. I'll be back to Taigh Mòr first and then off to see your father-in-law.'

'Send him our regards,' and with this Mrs Mackenzie threw a glance back towards the parlour. 'He's fallen out of favour with his father lately, but I've always found him a pleasant man wi a ready wit.'

'I will Mrs Mackenzie, I will. Good day to you.'

Cal hung back until Mrs Mackenzie had waved Muirhead off down the path and then he started after him, catching up at the cart and horse that stood in a sea of mud.

'A word?' Cal grabbed the Superintendent's sleeve. Muirhead shook Cal off.

'And you are?'

'Callum Robinson sir, from the *Philadelphia Star*.'

Muirhead looked perplexed. Cal went on.

'I'm sure you'll agree that a story like this can't be kept secret.'

'A secret? I wasn't aware it was a secret. Everyone round here knows about what happened'

'Well, not a secret perhaps. More like a cover-up.'

'A cover-up?' Muirhead raised his eyebrows. 'You're a reporter… and an American at that.'

'I am indeed, but don't let that prejudice you against me. I find so many people become closed mouthed when they hear my occupation announced.'

'I've nothing to say to you. I've already spoken to the *Highland News*.'

'I'm sure. But just for the record, what would you be wanting with this man Mackenzie?'

'I'm no at liberty to discuss this matter…'

'But you just said that everyone…'

'If you'll excuse me I have business to attend to,' and with that Muirhead climbed aboard the cart and indicated to the driver to move off.

'Sir, if you wouldn't mind…' Cal shouted

Muirhead dismissed the young newspaperman with a wave of his hand.

'You lousy… ah damn you.' Cal's words fell on deaf ears. The cart rapidly gained speed through the mud.

Cal narrowed his eyes against the daylight. Mrs Mackenzie stepped up softly behind him.

'He's important business to be about now, young man. He's no got time to answer your questions.' She steered Cal back inside the house and sat him down with a freshly brewed cup of tea.

'Explain.' Cal was rapidly losing his patience. 'And I don't want any more damned tea.' He pushed the proffered tea away roughly.

'Well now,' Mrs Mackenzie huffed. 'We'll have no more of that behaviour.'

'I'll behave exactly how I please.'

'Not while you're under my roof you won't.' Mrs Mackenzie began to clear the crockery.

She sounded just like my mother, Cal thought. God, my mother. What I would give to be back home right now. Maybe if I try a different tack. Buttered her up. I can do that. I can turn on the charm when I want.

'I'm sorry,' he said sullenly.

'Yes, well I should think so.'

'I haven't thanked you properly for looking after me in this way. I really am grateful.'

Mrs Mackenzie stopped what she was doing and sat down. She reached out and took Cal's hand in her own.

'You're about the same age as my John; Mr Mackenzie that is. Though you seem much younger, much more…' she struggled for the words. 'Immature.'

Cal withdrew his hand from her grasp.

'Oh I didn't mean anything by it, dear. It's just that I'm so much older than either of you. You're very alike you know. I think that's why I've taken such a shine to you.'

Cal smiled and patted her hand, leaving his own on top of hers now.

'Tell me what happened. What really happened.'

'Well now, dear, I shouldn't be gossiping you know.'

'Yes, but who's to hear?'

'Well there's Mr Mackenzie for a start. He'd not like it if he caught me tattle-telling.'

'Then we'll have to find somewhere more private, won't we? Somewhere where we won't be disturbed.' Cal looked directly into Mrs Mackenzie's eyes. Seducing an older woman, he thought. It's so easy. They fall for it every time.

'Oh no. No, no, no. That would never do. Never. No.' Mrs Mackenzie gave Cal a haughty glare and stood up.

Cal blinked innocently at her as if he didn't know what she meant.

'I know what you're about, young man. As much as I took a shine to you I know your sort. You're a charmer all right, that you are. A charmer. But you won't charm me. No. Not me. You'll forgive me if I take my leave of you now. I've a lot to do before tonight's festivities.'

Her rejection didn't appear to bother Cal in the slightest. Instead he hung onto her last few words: tonight's festivities. Hogmanay. That was it. He'd almost forgotten. If there was ever a time to get the gossip it was when the clans were gathering at Hogmanay.

'Will you have many guests?'

'Aye a fair few folk will drop by, but you'd be best advised to keep quiet about the goings on at the lighthouse now if you intend stopping a wee while.' She paused for a moment. 'You might consider how you're going to pay your bill too.'

'My valise is at a hotel in Stornoway.'

'Then you'd best be advised to send for it.'

Mrs Mackenzie busied herself with the breakfast crockery. She called out for the maid but when she didn't come the good lady of the house muttered something under her breath and left the room. Minutes later the maid entered, took one look at Cal and made to leave again.

'No, it's alright. You do your job,' he ventured. She was a pretty young thing. He caught a whiff of starch as she passed. She glanced at Cal coyly.

'There's talk that you're a reporter from America. Is that right?' Her accent was soft. Where had she learned her English?

'That's correct.'

She warmed to him slightly as she piled the plates.

'What are you reporting about?'

'The lighthouse.' Here was another opportunity. Milk it, boy, he thought. Milk it for all it's worth. He caught hold of her arm.

'I'll bet you hear a thing or two.'

She tugged her arm away gently.

'I might.'

'I'd make it worth your while.' Damn it, he needed more funds. He'd have to find a telegraph office. Tell Culpepper he was on to something big. Something huge in fact. Something that was about to blow sky high providing the locals didn't mess things up.

'What have you got that I might want now, mister?'

'That depends.'

She stared straight at him, her eyes glistening.

'On what?'

'On what you've heard. On what they're talking about.' Cal glanced around furtively before saying: 'Gossip.'

'Och, I hear gossip I do, sir. If all you want is gossip I hear it right enough.'

'Marie.' Mrs Mackenzie's voice rang out from the hallway. 'Don't be dawdling with those plates, and leave Mr Robinson alone. You're no to talk to him, do you hear me?'

Cal whispered conspiratorially to Marie: 'Ignore her.'

Marie giggled. Cal caught her hand again, this time holding it gently in his own. He inspected the bitten-down nails and the red raw skin.

'Look here now, a hand that needs kissing,' and he pressed it softly to his lips. Marie pulled away, embarrassed.

'I cannae.'

Cal sighed. 'Oh, but you can.' He paused to gauge her response. 'But that's not what I want right now.'

Marie stared at him.

'You're very beautiful. Too beautiful for this dump.'

Marie looked round in amazement.

'Why, this is the biggest house in these parts. It's a palace, it is.'

Cal laughed. 'Yeah a regular palace… and you its queen.'

'No,' she whispered.

'Yes.'

He blinked just as he had with Mrs Mackenzie. It spelled out his innocence, his charm, and his total insincerity.

'What d'you know about it?'

'They say a serpent took the lighthouse keepers.'

'Who does?'

'Och now, the old men that stop by for a wee dram.'

'A real serpent?'

'Aye. A real serpent. But I don't believe it myself.'

'Of course not.'

'It was terrible o course. Poor Joe.'

'Joe?'

'Aye, Joseph Moore. The lighthouse keeper that found them. Well no, not found them.'

'Not found them?'

'No. He just landed and went up to the lighthouse and they wasnae there anymore.' She looked wistfully out of the window.

'Captain Harvie came and sent a telegram way down at Calanais Farm there.'

'There's a telegraph office here?'

'Aye. We're no living in the back of beyond you know. We've modern equipment,' and she spoke as if she had personal knowledge of such 'modern equipment', though Cal couldn't possibly tell what else she might mean other than the telegraph. Nothing appeared very modern hereabouts.

'What about this Joseph Moore? What d'you know about him?'

'No much really. They keep themselves to themselves those lighthouse keepers. They never come here. They're away down at Taigh Mòr.'

That name again. He would have to check this Taigh Mòr out. Cal nodded, his ears pricked for further juicy titbits such gossip might render.

'Now Mrs Mackenzie now… well she gets down to Taigh Mòr on occasion because she's made friends wi Mrs Ducat.'

'Mrs Ducat?'

'Aye. The lighthouse keeper's wife.'

'Moore's wife?'

'No, no, no. The man in charge. Mr Ducat.'

'Mr Ducat.'

'Aye. He was one those poor souls that lost their life.'

'He died recently?'

'Are you stupid or something? He's one of the ones that was eaten by the sea serpent.'

'And you don't believe this?'

Marie sighed.

'Look here. Mr Ducat and two other men were lost from the island. And Joe found them missing.'

'He found them?'

'No. Och you're mad. I cannae talk to you.'

She waved her hand at him and picked up the plates, all pretence to shyness gone.

'Where would I find this Joseph Moore?'

Marie was almost out of the door. She stopped and turned back.

'At the lighthouse.' She shook her head.

The penny dropped, along with Cal's jaw. Joseph Moore. He was key to this. He was the man with a story to tell. Cal nodded and ran after Marie. He caught up with her in the entrance to the kitchen.

'Joseph Moore. How do I get to him? How do I talk to him?'

Marie sniffed.

'You didnae give me anything.'

'I haven't got time for games. How do I get to the lighthouse?'

Marie sneered. 'On a boat, you barm pot. On a boat.'

'Where from?'

Marie disappeared into the kitchen.

'Where from?' Cal shouted after her.

'Taigh Mòr.'

'Where the Superintendent was going?'

Marie ignored him, but Cal had his answer. He'd find a way out to the lighthouse at the shore station. That was where the boats went from for the Flannans – Taigh Mòr. He should have insisted on a ride with that Muirhead man. He would be miles away by now. Miles.

'Damn it,' he hissed. 'Damn it all.'

*

'Never thought I'd be spending Hogmanay in a lighthouse,' Archie Lamont muttered as he shovelled coal onto the fire. The light had faded fast and with it any warmth the day had offered.

'It's no so bad.' Milne smiled. 'O course you cannae get blind drunk. Not when you're on duty. But we can take a wee dram wi each other.'

The old sailor nodded.

'Aye, we can that. We can that.'

Joe stomped in. Cold air followed him and smoke swirled gently out of the fireplace. He took one look at Archie and went back outside again. He stood in the shelter of the wall, but when he heard the door slam he took off down the path towards the point. When he noticed Archie behind him, he veered off towards the Teampull. He hadn't wanted to return here, but it was on lower ground and night was cloaking his movements. He thought he might just head Archie off if he could reach the wall before the light swept round again.

The first thing Joe noticed about the old stones was that they felt warm to the touch. The second was a feeling of elation, as if he'd come home. He slipped inside and waited for any signs of Archie. When none came he relaxed a little and smiled.

Sanctuary. He'd found sanctuary.

It didn't last long. Archie's voice rang out.

'Are you there, laddie?'

Joe cursed. What did he want?

'Aye, I'm here.'

'You'll catch your death o cold.' Archie dipped inside the Teampull.

'It's peaceful.'

'It's bloody cold, that's what it is.'

'I was afraid for a while, but it's different now.'

'How so?'

'I'm next and I'm no afraid.'

Archie frowned.

Joe went on: 'I was always afraid o drowning. I cannae swim.'

'That's nothing surprising. There's no many sailors can swim.'

'No, I mean I can swim, but not good.'

Archie shrugged. 'I wouldnae worry about it.'

'No.' He paused, wondering if he could really trust this old sailor. What if he laughed at him? What if he didn't believe him?

'Since this happened I've been mortal afraid.' He glanced sideways at Archie, but he could barely see his face in the darkness.

'All my worst nightmares come to haunt me.'

'All mine are out at sea, laddie, but I have to find ways to ignore them or I wouldnae earn a living now would I?'

'No, no I suppose not.'

'I came here you know before; to the Teampull. I wanted to pay my dues to those old monks that lived here before we came and built the lighthouse.'

'But there's been no one living here for hundreds o years.'

'Exactly. No one has lived here for all that time and why I ask you? Why should that be so?'

'Well it's no exactly on the main route from Glasgow to Edinburgh now, is it? It's cold and bleak and there's nothing here much but sea birds.'

'Aye, and isn't that exactly what St Kilda's like?'

'True.'

'And there's people there alright.'

'Aye.'

'So why not here? There used to be. I've seen the houses on Eilean Tighe. There's houses here too. Mounds in the grass now, but places where man lived. I know I've said before about this. I know I sounded like I knew what had happened, but I didnae. Not at all.'

'St Kilda's a dying place. Maybe that's what happened here.'

Joe shook his head. 'No. 'Til recent they kept sheep here from Lewis.'

'Aye, some.'

'And they took them off and didnae come back.'

'No. You're right. They didnae come back.'

They fell silent. In the space the silence created between them Joe felt the ground fall away. The thick walls of the Teampull closed in. The chasm grew narrow and dark, and the air colder.

'Are you still there, Archie?'

'Aye, I'm here.' But Archie's voice seemed faint. As if he was speaking from a great distance away.

Joe reached out to find the older man, and did indeed feel the softness of cloth beneath his grasp, but when he put his hand up to touch Lamont's face the old sailor grabbed his hand and held it fast. Or at least that was what Joe thought. When a hiss came soft in his ear he wasn't so sure.

'Welcome.' That was all the voice said, but it wasn't Archie Lamont. Oh no, not Archie. Joe stepped back and wrenched his hand from the vice-like grip.

'Where are you?'

Silence, but for his own laboured breath.

'Archie? Don't…'

There was someone else here. Not Lamont. Not one of the other lighthouse keepers. Someone else.

'Who is it?' He thought he said it out loud. He waited; held his breath. Listened. Listened to the wind outside. Listened to the sea. Listened to the hum of roosting birds and grunts from the seals. He listened hard and when he was almost done listening and had drummed up the courage to leave he heard the voice again.

'Sacrifice.'

The word sent chills to the very core of his being.

'Leave me alone.' But the words were only thoughts that raced in his head and weren't spoken out loud, though he thought he'd said them. He could have sworn he'd said them.

'Sacrifice, that you may be set free.'

Joe covered his ears. Closed his eyes. Where was Lamont? Where was he?

'No, no. I'm not afraid. Go away. Leave me be. I've done nothing. I've done nothing at all. It wasn't my fault.' This time the words echoed loud.

'Whose fault was it then?' It was Lamont's voice now, cutting through the piercing darkness, the noise-filled silence.

'Archie? I thought…'

Joe stumbled forward.

'Here laddie. There now. Dinnae fret. I lost you in the dark and must've stepped outside. I couldnae find the entrance.'

'It's lighter now.'

'Aye, the moon was hid behind a cloud but the weather's clearing a little, at least for now. What was you saying before? About it being your fault. I didnae catch it.'

'Nothing. No, nothing much.' Joe felt stupid now. There was no way Lamont would understand or believe him. 'Go back. I want to be on my own for a while.'

'Are you sure?'

'Aye, I'm sure.'

'Alright then, laddie, alright.' The darkness had indeed lifted a little and Joe could just make Lamont out through the grey light. After a while he was alone again. He wondered why he'd chosen to stay when he'd been so afraid only moments earlier. A sacrifice that he might be set free. Did it mean his death? Or did it mean that he would survive if he could sacrifice… someone else? But who? It couldn't be murder. He wouldn't have that on his hands. He doubted he could kill anything let alone another human being.

A sacrifice.

Blood libation. He remembered. That's what they did here. They offered blood. He knew when he re-enacted the ceremony that he'd forgotten something. Thrice round, a deisal turn, that meant sunwise, and do it naked, then enter the building on your knees. That's what he'd done. That's what the old book had said. The one he'd left at the shore station. But it had been a while since he'd read it and then only half-heartedly to fill time – and he'd forgotten the blood libation.

The sacrifice.

It came to him suddenly: his soul would be set free only if he could offer up someone else's in exchange.

'Sacrifice.' The word escaped from his mouth and this time his voice rang out. He couldn't kill anyone and who would agree to offer themselves to the sea, to the ancients, to the ghostly presence, to the phantom? He couldn't think of anyone that would be willing to do this for him. He knew of no one who was that stupid. Yes, that's what this sacrifice business was – stupid. He was doomed then. Doomed.

*

The girl Marie had told Cal it was only a couple of miles or so to Taigh Mòr. He reasoned that it might only take him half an hour or so to get there on foot, and then again it might take much longer. He returned to his room, inspected his shoes, and decided that although they were the worse for wear after his recent jaunt across Scotland, they would have to last him a little while longer. If the road thus far was anything to go by then his onward journey would be no less difficult. His other problem was that he wasn't sure if he would be able to procure a safe passage out to the Flannans on this particular day, it being Hogmanay, but he thought he'd give it a damned good try. At least he had somewhere to stay. If all else failed he would return to Garynahine and continue to question the locals.

Decisions made, Cal readied his few possessions, and started out for Breascleit. A few hundreds yards down the road and he was already having misgivings. The so-called road was naught but a continuation of the muddy track. He faired no better on the verge, which was mostly squelchy peat interspersed with rocks. Half an hour stretched into an hour and a half, then two hours and finally, when his feet were wet through and he'd broken into a cold sweat beneath his layers of jacket and overcoat, he spied the first Breascleit houses.

The short day had faded and lights showed in a few of the windows. Buoyed by the thought that he was nearing the source of his story, Cal pressed forward with renewed vigour. The black houses melted into the landscape, now greying as the night closed in. The road firmed up some and a well-built stone wall outlined the garden of the shore station. Cal lent on this wall to get his breath back, wiped his forehead with the sleeve of his coat, and noticed a woman coming towards him from the other direction. She had two children at her heels and was carrying a basket. Cal stepped forward as she levelled with him.

'May I offer my assistance?'

The woman cocked her head and looked at him quizzically, then with a hint of a Cockney accent said: 'You're an American.'

Cal was somewhat taken aback. It was a statement of fact and he hadn't expected to hear what he reckoned was almost 'proper' English issuing from the mouth of a Hebridean woman. The children ran through the gate and up the path. Annie Macarthur glanced back at Cal as he watched her follow them.

'Yes,' Cal mumbled. 'I'm an Am…'

Annie walked on up to the door. He could hear the rustle of her skirts and briefly imagined her legs hidden beneath.

'Callum Robinson,' he went on, opening the gate for himself now.

Annie stopped. 'That's a Scottish name.'

'Correct.'

They eyed each other in the closing darkness.

'You're in mourning,' Cal observed, though why this should come to him when half the women he'd met wore black he didn't rightly know.

Annie nodded assent.

'Might I offer my condolences?'

'Thank you kindly, sir.'

Cal shuffled and then ventured: 'Your husband?'

Annie nodded again.

Cal imagined a tear in her eye and wanted to brush it away, but he held back from reaching out to her.

'So you would be married to one of the lighthouse men?' It was a leap in the dark he knew, and one that could backfire, but he reckoned he was beyond worrying if he'd made some terrible faux pas or not.

'I'm a widow now.'

'Yes, a widow.'

'I have to go in. Please excuse me.'

This time Cal was the one to nod. Annie disappeared inside. Cal stood on the path for a moment, and then he knocked on the same door. A small girl opened it a bit and peeped out.

'Yes,' she said in a singsong voice.

'I've come about the lighthouse.'

'We're no the lighthouse, mister. We're the shore station.'

'Yes, no. I mean...'

'Are you here about what happened?'

Annabella opened the door a wee bit more and stuck her foot out into the opening. Cal noticed her sturdy laced shoes were well polished and felt ashamed of his own muddy footwear.

'A lady entered here a moment ago.'

'Who? Annie? I mean, Mrs Macarthur?'

Cal wasn't sure. He said yes anyway.

'She's no a lady. Don't you know that? A lady is someone aristo...aristo...'

'Cratic?'

'Yes. That. Aristocratic. Annie....' here Annabella shook her head. 'I mean Mrs Macarthur is no a lady. She's a Mrs.'

'I suspect you're right.'

'I know I'm right.'

Cal smiled unconvincingly at her. My, but she was a horror.

'Well, can I talk to her?'

'Oh I expect so, if you come in. Do you want to come in the now?'

'That would be the general idea.'

'Aye, well I'll have to ask my Mama. Wait there,' and just like that she closed the door and left him standing there wondering what the conversation had been about. A few moments later the door opened again. Annie Macarthur stood on the threshold.

Cal was momentarily flustered. She was beautiful. Even in the half-light he could tell that, despite what the little brat of a girl had said, he was in the presence of a lady.

'She called you by name. You're her mother?'

Annie shook her head.

'No.'

'Ah.'

'What exactly do you want?'

'This is Taigh Mòr right?'

'It is.'

'You must be heartbroken.'

'You could put it like that. But you didn't answer my question.'

Cal licked his lips. He was just warming up.

'You're Mrs Macarthur?'

'Yes.'

'So your husband is one of the missing keepers?'

'I believe we have already had this conversation.' Annie turned away to close the door, but Cal put his hand out and stopped her.

'I have come a very long way for this story.' He sounded frustrated. 'And I won't go away empty-handed. Not now. Not after the things I've heard about sea serpents and the like.'

'Sea serpents?'

Cal noted the alarm in Annie's voice.

'What about sea serpents?'

'Some are saying that sea serpents took the men off the lighthouse. Now, I don't know if this is true or not, but I sure would like to find out.'

'Sea serpents. Why they're what you read about in books, aren't they? They aren't real.'

'Ah, well. I couldn't say, Ma'am. I couldn't say. But if I could just come in for one moment I'm sure we could discuss it further.'

'I don't know. I'll have to ask Mrs Ducat. Sea serpents you say. My, oh, my.' Annie cautioned him: 'Wait there.'

This time the door remained open and Cal couldn't resist stepping over the threshold. He scanned the layout of the hall quickly, taking in the dark wood panelling, the coat stand, the mirror on the wall next the front door, the stairs off and the darker back hall. A door to the right opened and Annabella dashed out, quickly followed by Annie, who beckoned Cal to come forward. He was ushered into the parlour. A woman sat by the fire, her legs covered with a plaid blanket. Her face was drawn, her skin colour ivory save for the dark circles around her eyes. These she raised to the newcomer. In that moment Cal felt a knife-sharp stab of icy cold cut through his heart. He put his hand to his chest and swayed. Annie caught him and he sank into an armchair.

'You're ill, man. You should have said. What are you doing out when you're ill?'

'I'm sorry. I'll be fine. Just fine. I've had a chill of late, that's all.' It was something of an understatement. He glanced up. The other woman had a faraway look in her eyes. Annie settled down next to her and took her hands up in her own. She smiled bleakly.

'Mrs Ducat and I would appreciate it if you would tell us about the sea serpents,' she said.

'There's nothing much to tell. I don't believe in them myself.'

Mary looked up. Her lips were cracked and a deathly blue.

'You don't believe in them?'

'No, Ma'am. They're the stuff of fantasy. What happened to those men… well who can tell?'

Mary nodded.

'Yet if people are talking about sea serpents there must be something in it surely?' she asked, turning to Annie for confirmation. Gently, Annie brushed a wisp of hair out of her friend's eyes.

Cal scratched his head.

'When did you see your husband last?'

Mary blinked, unable to answer.

'It was the seventh of December, wasn't it?' Annie put her arm round Mary's shoulder and looked directly at Cal as if challenging him to say differently. 'It was the seventh.'

'And that goes for your husband too, does it?'

'I haven't seen Donald for a long while now.'

'Ah, Donald. Who were the keepers exactly?' Cal slipped his notebook out. He headed a new page 'Lighthouse Mystery Solved'.

'James Ducat, Principal Keeper. Thomas Marshall, Keeper, and Donald Macarthur, Occasional,' Annie replied.

'Occasional? What does that mean?'

'He wasn't really a keeper. He was a stonemason and a tailor.'

Cal looked up from his notes. Mary had begun to weep, quite silently but forcefully. Annie held onto her tightly as if letting her go might mean total collapse for them both. Cal sensed that asking more questions would be unfeeling and yet he also knew that if he didn't probe further, when both women were at their most vulnerable, he might lose the opportunity for this kind of raw emotion. If he could capture this grief, exposing these women's fragility in doing so, then he would have a wonderful story to sell to his editor. He pressed on.

'How d'you get to be an "Occasional" if you're a stone-mason and, you say, a tailor?' The two did not seem compatible occupations.

'My Donald was a rare man. He'd been in the English navy so he had.'

'Had he indeed? And so James Ducat was your husband, Ma'am,' he said pointing his notebook at Mary. She didn't reply so he continued. 'Who is er... Thomas Marshall's wife then?'

'He isn't...wasn't married,' Annie mumbled.

'He must have had someone.'

'His father. And a sister.'

'Uhuh. And how do you feel right now? Now you know you'll never see... er.... ' He referred to his notes. 'Donald, again.'

Neither woman answered him. Annie stared off into space. Mary had sunk inward, as if her vital organs had collapsed and she had become a hollow shell.

At last Annie whispered. 'We shouldn't have asked you in. Leave us be.'

But Cal wasn't going to be put off the scent now he was so close to that truly unique moment; the moment he called privately the 'magic minute'. It was this magic minute that he was striving to force the women to face; a moment when they would hand him the ultimate quote. He wouldn't leave until that had happened. He stepped his questions up.

'What was going through your mind when you heard the news that they were missing? They were missing weren't they? I mean you didn't just hear that they were dead? Not just like that.' He said it in a deliberately uncaring way. Their grief wasn't his. Sympathy wasn't a word he was used to other than as a throwaway comment. And the beautiful one that had been married to Donald, she was close to his precious magic minute. He thought the other was already too far-gone. No point in pressing her for anything else, but this one – Annie wasn't it? She still had fight in her. She would give him the magic minute. She may even give him much more.

'Ma'am? Who was it told you they were dead? They are dead, aren't they? They aren't coming back? No… maybe sea serpents did get them after all.' Cal gave a chuckle. 'Sea serpents eh? Who'd have thought?'

'No. No more. Please leave us.'

'I understand. You're grieving. But you see this is a wonderful opportunity. How many can say they've lost loved ones to sea serpents?'

'No,' Annie's voice was louder now. The magic minute was close. So close.

'Sea serpents are rare creatures. I'd love to be persuaded that they exist. What a story that would be.'

'You must leave us. We don't have anything more to say.'

'But you must have. What you must be going through I can't begin to imagine. You have to tell me. You have to help me understand.'

'You can't possibly ever understand. Ever. To kiss your husband goodbye one day and watch him take the steamer out to the island and then to wait… and wait… and then… to know that he won't ever come back. He won't ever, ever… come back…. And the pain. The pain here in my heart,' and here Annie thumped her breast bone hard so that it sounded hollow. 'How can you ever know? You have no right to come here and ask these questions. You have no right. Who are you? Who? What are you doing here? You talk about sea serpents, but you don't know what it's like to live with a man whose blood runs thick with the sea. You don't know. They aren't just stories. Not to folks here. They're as real as you and me. And if that's what's happened to my Donald, then that's what's happened. You understand?'

Cal didn't reply. He just raised his eyebrows.

'Do you understand me? If it was sea serpents that took them then it was sea serpents and don't you tell me otherwise.' Annie sat down, the wind gone from her sails.

This was the moment Cal had bargained for, that Annie would either fall totally silent or reply to every single question he asked hereafter.

'There was a man here today. A Superintendent Muirhead. I believe he was headed out to somewhere called Mevaig. Where is he now?'

'You missed him He's gone already.' Annie answered now in a voice devoid of emotion.

'Aha. And d'you expect him back here?'

'Briefly, before he returns to Edinburgh.'

'Who is this Roderick Mackenzie I've heard about at Garynahine?'

'He was meant to keep lookout for the light. He was given a telescope to do the job properly.' Annie looked out of the window. Cal followed her gaze.

'Lonely place. You don't belong here, do you?'

'I come from faraway.' Her voice carried longing in it that caught Cal's attention for just a moment too long.

It was getting hot in here. Must be too close to the fire, he thought, and he stood up and walked to the window placing his hand against the glass to catch the cold air from outside.

'I might go home now,' Annie said quietly.

'Home,' Cal echoed. She was right – home was far, far away. He sighed.

'I have to get out to the lighthouse. How do I do that?'

Annie didn't say anything and he took a dizzying step towards her, feeling the heat once more. He couldn't tell if it was the temperature in the room or a fever.

'The pier, I suppose. Or…'

'Think, woman.'

'I don't know. Er… you could try the bothan.'

'The bothan.'

'Yes, it's where the men gather of an evening. But it's Hogmanay.'

'Then they'll all be there won't they? Where's this bothan?'

'Back up the road you came on. It's just a tumbledown black house.'

Mary reached out.

'No good'll come of it, son,' she said.

Cal scowled. He'd had enough. He felt fevered and confined and for the first time in a while he needed a drink. The bothan sounded like just the place to find one.

He nodded his head towards the two women and said: 'It's been a pleasure, ladies. A real pleasure.' After all that he couldn't get out fast enough.

The coldness of the air caught him unawares. Nevertheless, a sweat broke out on his forehead, which grew worse with every step he took. His hands felt clammy too, and the dizziness he'd felt inside had also remained with him. He leant on the wall for a moment before setting off for the pier. At first the road was fringed with wide verges that gave onto the fields but further along the road narrowed and dug deep between houses that to Cal seemed to just grow from the earth itself.

Close to the pier a group of women watched his progress. He staggered like a drunk, coughing and spluttering into his sleeve. They watched until he was within earshot, then they feigned disinterest.

He hailed them loudly: 'Ladies.'

They didn't respond. He tried to smile, unaware that his dishevelled appearance gave him the air of a tramp.

The women turned their backs on him and melted into the growing darkness. Cal teetered at the edge of the pier, gazing down into the water. It looked cool and inviting. He was just about to step off into the sweet deep calmness when an old man grabbed him by the arm and yanked him back. Cal glimpsed deep-set beady eyes in a weather-beaten face.

'I know who you are,' the old man exclaimed, his hand still clutching Cal's arm.

'Who?'

'You. I know who you are. You're that reporter fellow. Are you no?'

Cal replied wearily. 'Yes.'

'You want to meet the fellow that's left?'

'What fellow?' Riddles, always riddles.

The old man leant in close and whispered the name loudly in Cal's ear.

'Joseph Moore.'

'Yes. Can you help me?' Cal turned on the old man and grabbed him by the lapels, shaking him as hard as he could, given that he was weak from his illness.

'I might and I might not.'

Money, it always came down to money.

'What d'you want?' Cal felt around in his pocket. He didn't have much money on him. He'd left most of it in his valise back in Stornoway. He pulled out a few coins. What did they use for money here?

'I don't know. What d'you want?' he repeated.

'Well now, what have you got?'

Cal held the coins out to him.

'Can you take me there?'

'Where?'

'To the lighthouse.'

'Aye, but it'll cost you mind. It's a long way across the sea to Flannan. It'll waste the evening that it will.'

Cal searched his pockets in vain.

'I've more. Do you know Mrs Mackenzie at Garynahine?'

'Aye, not well mind. She knows me though. Donald the Boat I am. Aye, Donald the Boat.'

'She'll reimburse you.'

'She'll what now?'

'She'll give you the money. If I write you a note for her.'

'Och, I don't know now.' Donald the Boat started to walk away.

'Please. I'll write it out now,' and Cal fetched his notebook and tore a page from it. He scribbled out a note asking Mrs Mackenzie to give the bearer the money she would find in his valise when it came from Stornoway. He thrust the note at Donald, who looked at it quizzically before he stuffed it in his pocket.

'Aye well, she's a wee tub, she is, but she'll get you there.'

He pointed to a boat that bobbed next to three others in the tiny bay. Clearly he meant Cal to take himself out to the lighthouse. Realising this Cal shook his head.

'You take me.'

'Och now there's no enough money in the world for me to take you out there on Hogmany.'

Cal brought out his pocket watch – the one his father had given him for his twenty-first birthday. He held it out. Donald the Boat grabbed at it greedily, turned it over in his hands and made smacking noises with his lips.

'Well now, we'll have to start right away. Aye right away.'

Cal wrapped his coat tight around his frail body. Now he was getting somewhere.

'Lead on, old man,' he said.

Donald the Boat gave Cal a gap-toothed grin.

ELEVEN

༄

Four sets of elbows rested on the lighthouse kitchen table. Tobacco smoke lent a gentle fog to the atmosphere. Four glasses and a bottle of whisky stood on the table between the men that sat there: John Milne, Donald Jack, Joseph Moore and Archie Lamont. The rain sounded soft against the windowpane, like someone tapping on the glass with gloves on.

Joe fastened his eyes on the bottle. He'd never been a drinker. He knew the consequences of starting down that track. Right now though he'd like a drink. He imagined the fiery liquid burning his throat, anaesthetising his existence.

'It doesn't feel like New Year,' Archie said.

Joe shook his head. No, it didn't. Not like New Year at all. Last year things had been different. The lighthouse had been brand new. It had only been lit since the seventh of

December. There was a photograph somewhere. The lighthouse all decked out with flags and Principal Keeper Ducat standing there smiling for the camera. The wind had been blowing as usual. Joe hadn't been here then. He hadn't come out to the new lighthouse until the twenty-first. A whole year since he'd first set foot on the Flannans. Joe shuddered as if someone had just walked over his grave.

Milne and Jack exchanged glances. It was hard for them but in a different way. They hadn't been here long and could get on with their routines. The men's disappearance wasn't affecting them as it did Joe. Still, they couldn't help but feel the atmosphere.

'Donnie man, would you take a drink wi me,' Archie asked, and he picked up the bottle and poured a shot of whisky into one of the glasses. Donald Jack nodded.

'John?'

'Aye, I'll take one the now, but no more mind. I'm on duty.'

'Joe?'

Joe shook his head, no. He would wait. He wanted a drink like nothing on earth, but he would wait. There was plenty of time before midnight. He didn't want to get drunk just yet. He couldn't be sure that once he started he wouldn't just carry on. It was important to retain some control now, but it wasn't like the control he'd always struggled with before. No, this was a resignation to fate that had mysteriously given him a calm power.

'Go on, laddie. Take a wee dram wi me. I'll be offended otherwise,' Archie smiled. It was hard to think of Archie getting offended by anyone. Joe felt his heart buoyed by the old man's presence.

'Aye, alright then. A small one mind.'

Archie poured the golden liquid out slowly, easily; the light from the fire reflected off the glass.

'Thank you,' Joe muttered and reached out to take it. In that moment he caught a movement out of the corner of his eye and turned in time to see the kitchen door open slowly. No one else noticed. He made to get up and push the door closed but Archie touched his arm.

'What about a game of cards?'

'I'd best close the door.'

Archie twisted round in his seat.

'It's shut tight, laddie.'

No, no it wasn't. It was standing open. Joe turned and saw that yes, the door was indeed closed. It's alright, he thought. It was just a trick of the light, that was all.

Donald Jack shuffled the cards and placed them in the centre of the table so they could be cut. Joe reached forward and again glimpsed a movement. The room had become darker now; only the table held any light. Even the fire in the grate had burnt away, the coals glowing red, the smoke curling convoluted spirals up the chimney. Shadowy figures roamed the dark fringes of the room. Nervously, Joe cut the cards.

'What'll we play?' he asked, keeping his voice steady, mindful of the fact that he had seen and felt a lot of things lately that no one else seemed to experience. He saw Archie frown, noticed the other two men watched him closely. Perhaps more closely than he would have liked.

'Gin rummy? Are you no going to play wi me?' he ventured nervously. It was important to appear normal. Whatever normal was. Joe certainly wasn't sure anymore.

'Aye laddie, we'll play.' Archie indicated that Donald should deal the cards.

Joe felt a prickle of hairs on the back of his neck. He daren't look round. He didn't need to. He could feel their presence. He knew they were with him now – the three men – his fellow lighthouse keepers. Not those seated with him at the table, but his dead compatriots. They stood in the shadows – their faces in the half-light – their eyes black pits of doom. Water dripped from their oilskins onto the floor. Only the ill-fated Donald Macarthur stood in his shirtsleeves, his fists clenched tight, ribboned veins standing out on his neck and along the taut muscles of his forearms.

Joe licked his lips and stood up very slowly, very carefully. He must keep a check on his emotions. It was vitally important not to let the other three men know about these ghosts. He didn't want to be branded a mad man. It would be the end of him. The end.

'Where are you going, laddie?' Archie asked. 'Sit down. Take another drink wi us. I thought you wanted to play cards.'

'No, I'm fine the now. I think I'll get a breath of fresh air.'

The ghostly apparitions filed out of the kitchen. Joe followed after. Outside he paused to get the measure of his companions, but they were way ahead of him on the path down to the west landing. Should he follow them? Joe wasn't sure. What if they led him to his death? What then? Or perhaps… perhaps that was what was meant to happen.

They were waiting for him to catch up. He started out after them and they turned in unison and continued on their way. By the time Joe reached the top of the west landing the three men were stepping out into the void beyond the cliffs. One by one the night swallowed them. Joe teetered on the brink, grabbed a hold of the railings, and started down the steps. No, not now. Not yet. The time wasn't right. It would be soon, but not now. Not on New Year's Eve. Not with a storm brewing and the light shining a reminder that he had a job to do.

*

The little boat barely appeared to move through the choppy sea. Cal felt sick to his stomach but he gripped the side and set his jaw. He was going to get his scoop. He was close now. Very close – and he could actually see the light. There it was on the horizon. It was small; no more than a brightness really that blinked on and off, on and off as it revolved, but it was there.

Donald the Boat struggled to keep his craft in line with his destination. Cal hunched his shoulders deeper and braved the drenching they got each time they dipped into the waves. His chest felt as tight as a drum and his head was pounding. He would get this story, *his* story. He would get it if it killed him.

'How long?' he asked the old man.

'Och now, a while yet. Aye, a good wee while.'

*

A cold light filtered in through the bedroom window. Joe cracked open an eye. His breath had misted the glass overnight. All in all he'd slept rather well. His bunk was comfortable. His feet were warm. His hands curled into soft fists that he stretched and recurled, like a cat waking from a lazy dream in the sun. He yawned. Time enough to worry. His lids fluttered. Sleep took him back.

*

They'd been at sea almost ten hours. For a long while the light got no closer and then suddenly the first of the Flannans loomed large to port. Cal mustered all his strength to sit upright and greet his destination. Donald the Boat nodded towards Eilean Tighe.

'That's no the one. It's t'other.'

Cal could see that.

'How long?'

'How long, how long. Can you no ask anything else?'

*

The ghosts stepped out into the darkness and the sea washed over them and took them out past the rocks at the mouth of the inlet, past the rocks where the seal basked in the summer, past the wash of water over the little island in the distance. The waves cradled their bodies and rocked them way, way out into the viscous grey Atlantic.

Joe turned over and pulled the blanket high up under his chin.

'There's a boat! Joe, wake yourself. There's a boat coming!'

The voice came from a long way away.

'Joe. Come on, will you?'

Joe woke with a start. Archie was standing over him.

'A wee fragile thing. Milne's down there the now. Rouse yourself and come help.'

Joe struggled to pull himself together.

'Are they in trouble?'

'I cannae tell. Come on, laddie. Make haste'

*

Milne threw a line down to Donald the Boat and tied off. His boots slipped on the slimy stone. The morning tide was still low, the swell as yet a gentle sweep of water in and out of the inlet.

Joe reached the top of the steps and started down, Archie following close on his heels.

'Who is it?' he shouted, but his voice was lost to the wind. He could see a huddled figure in the stern of the tiny boat. Milne reached down and helped Donald the Boat clamber up.

'Are you mad? That's no steamer you have there.'

'You may say that. Aye, you may. But my family have been at sea for centuries. I reckon as I know these waters like the back of my hand.'

Archie slapped the intrepid sailor on the back.

'Och man. It's Donald the Boat is it no? I've no seen you for a while. Are you well?'

'Aye, I am that. A wee bit put out for having to come all this way on Hogmanay. You wouldnae have a wee dram about the place, would you?'

'I think we can find that for you,' Archie glanced down into the boat where the bedraggled man was attempting to stand up.

'Give him a hand out, Joe.'

At the name Cal looked up. For one moment Joe stared deep into the black heart of Cal's soul. Their eyes locked and Joe felt the world momentarily spin away from him. There was danger here with this man. Great danger. He didn't know what but he couldn't be around him.

He turned quickly to Donald the Boat. 'Who is he?'

'Some newspaperman. Paid me more money than you've set eyes on. Gave me a promissory note to give to Mrs Mackenzie at Garynahine he did. Honest woman that Mrs Mackenzie, and no short o the funds to make this right if he turns out to be lying through his eyeteeth. She'll pay up. I'll make sure o that.' He tipped his head at Cal. ''Tween you and me, I think he's a mad man. More money than sense. Mind, I wouldnae stop him spending it. A wee dram and then I'm away back to collect my earnings.'

Milne helped Cal up onto the landing. He could barely stand, but his eyes were hungry as he took everything in.

'You cannae leave her moored like this,' Joe said to Donald the Boat. 'You'll have to get away soon. He cannae stay wi us.'

'Och, now. I'm no taking him back. He hasn't paid for that.'

Joe started up the steps after Donald the Boat and Archie. 'You cannae leave him here wi us.'

Leaning heavily on John Milne, Cal attempted a half-hearted smile.

'You're Joseph Moore,' he muttered feebly.

'What of it?'

'I'm here for your story.'

*

An hour later Donald the Boat set out eastwards for the shores of Lewis and home. He left Cal sitting in front of the kitchen fire, a blanket wrapped around his shoulders, a cup of hot sweet tea cupped in his hands. Archie had offered the newspaperman the whisky but he'd shook his head, no. Cal couldn't stop shivering. Couldn't stop the pounding in his head. Couldn't stop the pain in his chest, or the fits of coughing where blood came up instead of phlegm. Drink wouldn't do it, not now. Maybe not ever again.

They'd been kind to him, he supposed. They'd said he could stay until the tender came. The one called Archie had said it would be any day now. He wasn't really a lighthouse keeper at all. He was a sailor. The others were lighthouse keepers. They would stay behind. They… Argh… it all became a red hazy blur.

'I don't want to die without I get the story,' he muttered. But there was no one in the kitchen to listen. They were off somewhere. It didn't matter. The only one he was interested in was Joseph Moore.

Joseph Moore.

He said it out loud several times until it became the spell that bound him to get up and find the man whose name he'd uttered. Rising from the chair, he steadied himself on the table. He banged the cup down on the surface and staggered to the door.

*

Joe could feel Cal's presence at his back as he stood on the cliffs above the west landing, though the newspaperman was wrapped in a blanket and out of sight. The tide had turned and the wind whipped ropes of foam off the crest of each wave. So far the rain was holding off, save for a slight spittle that came with each gust, but Joe could feel the storm gathering momentum out in the greying Atlantic and wondered just how much longer he would have to be here before his transfer came through. His leaving seemed all the more important since this stranger had arrived. Perhaps especially since this stranger had arrived. But even as he thought this he knew that leaving the Flannans would not release the phantom's hold on him. He worried that it would dog him all his life.

'If only there was a way,' and he meant a way to offer up the blood libation – the sacrifice. He shuddered. There was this man of course – this newspaperman. Maybe he... no. Don't think of that. But what did he really want? Was it as he said? The story of how the men came to be missing and how he, Joe, found the place deserted? Was that what this Callum Robinson really wanted? Or was he here for more sinister reasons? Joe wondered if some all-powerful force, now controlling his destiny in ways he could only begin to guess, had sent this stranger.

'Callum Robinson,' he said into the wind. It was a Scottish name. A good old Scottish name. But he wasn't Scottish was he, this man? He was an American. And he was obsessed. Anyone could see that. Coming out here in a boat like the one poor old Donald the Boat sailed; a ruined old thing that might capsize in the slightest of swells. That was sheer folly. No, it was obsession pure and simple. It couldn't be anything else. But what if this stranger had been sent to fulfil the blood libation? What then?

'No,' Joe shouted. He couldn't do that. He shook the thoughts from his mind. No, not that.

The sea rolled in slowly; wave feeding wave, the undertow only visible when each breaker sucked back from the rocks over which they washed ferociously. At this height it was an easy thing to fall prey to vertigo. There was no way Joe could kill someone else, but he wondered if he could kill himself. It would take an immense amount of strength to do the deed – to jump deliberately. Yet it was an easy thing for a man to fall, to slip. No one would notice for a while. By the time they had missed him his body would be washed away. Just like the keepers. He took the stone out of his pocket and looked at it. No, he couldn't do that either. He couldn't deliberately kill himself. It required a braver man than he. Besides suicide was cheating. 'Felo de se' they used to call it. Self-murder.

The blood libation. The only way out of this nightmare other than to leave the island right here and now, and he wouldn't be able to do that until the tender returned. They'd told Cal it wouldn't be long, but they knew it could be weeks. He could be stranded here with a man that had been sent to drain his very spirit from him. It was all so confusing.

And then it came to him: not suicide, but fate. He would simply wait here for the waves to wash in and take him away, as had happened with the keepers. He wasn't afraid. He felt strangely elated. Death wasn't something he needed to fear. It would come anyway, whether he lay awake worrying about it or not. Best make the most of it then. Die as the others had died. Escape the island and his fears by riding it out. Challenge death to take him. Challenge the waves to take him. Yes, it was so simple. So perfect.

Blood libation.

Not suicide.

Not murder.

Just fate, and why should he fear destiny?

*

Cal wore dry clothing and was wrapped in the thick grey blanket, but when he stepped outside he still felt the cold creep in. Every bone in his body hurt. Every muscle felt torn and bruised. It hurt to breathe. It hurt to open his eyes, but he wouldn't be put off his prey. The story was so close, so very close. This man Joseph Moore, what a mystery he was. Why, he hadn't spoken more than a handful of words since Cal had landed, and now here he was gazing out to sea atop a cliff that looked too dangerous to traverse even when it wasn't blowing a gale.

'Come inside, laddie,' Archie called to Cal from the kitchen.

Cal ignored him. Since his arrival this old man had done nothing but ask questions. That, and mollycoddle him like a woman.

Cal hiked the blood from the back of his throat and spat it out onto the path. He screwed his eyes up and took a tentative step towards the cliffs. The wind took away what little breath he had. He tripped on the blanket, stumbled, yet managed somehow to right himself. His quarry was in sight.

*

Joe had been watching a series of waves for some time, random thoughts about destiny running through his mind, remnants of memories mixed up with fantasy. But although he'd been watching these waves he'd not really been concentrating. They had hypnotised him by their incessant rolling and rolling, the swell now easy, now vertical, tendrils of kelp caught at the world's end as the sea lashed hard against the island. This being the case he didn't notice Cal come up behind him, not with his conscious mind anyway. And then it was too late to escape the newspaperman and his obsession. He was here on the steps, the blanket caught on a stone behind him. His eyes red raw and wild.

Joe waited for the inevitable questioning to begin. He didn't know that Cal had used every last ounce of strength left in him to reach the cliffs, but when he staggered and sought out the railings with his cold hand Joe couldn't help but reach out and steady him.

'You should be inside. It's madness to be here in this weather.'

Cal coughed out the words: 'Why are you then?'

'I'm paid to do this.'

'But not to risk your life.'

'It comes with the territory.'

Cal tried to wave Joe away, but couldn't stand unaided.

'I can manage. I'm not at death's door yet.'

'There's some as would argue otherwise.' Joe felt the claw-like grip of the newspaperman's hand on his arm.

'Tell me what you saw.'

Joe broke Cal's grasp. The railings stopped him from falling to his death.

'Nothing.'

'You must have seen something. You were the first man here. You must have felt it.'

'Felt what?'

'This place. Everything here feels like death. Everything here smells like death.' Cal broke out in a fit of coughing. Flecks of blood spotted his chin.

Joe shrugged. Why should he give his innermost secret thoughts away?

'I talked to their wives. They told me about you. That one with the sweet face, she told me about you. What was her name now? Mrs Macarthur. Yes, that was it.'

'What did she tell you?' Joe feared the worse; thought that Annie might have mentioned his desire for her. No. He shook his head. That wasn't possible. She wouldn't do something like that. She wouldn't tell a stranger about something they'd kept a secret even from each other.

Cal spat into the wind.

'You were partial to her then?'

'No. She's Donald's wife,' and then Joe remembered that Donald was dead. Gone. Washed away, Muirhead had said, by a freak wave. Drowned; his body battered and bloated by now. He caught Cal eyeing him with relish. What a miserable excuse for a man.

'You were sweet on her alright.' Cal chuckled and it came up from his chest like a death rattle. 'The old man Archie thinks you're going mad you know.'

'And you're no mad for coming here? In this weather. In that boat? Putting that poor old soul's life in danger. Do you no ken how dangerous these rocks are? Have you no idea, man, what could have happened to you?'

Cal didn't reply. Instead both men listened to the swell and suck of water in the rocky inlet. When Cal did speak it was to ask about the sea serpent.

'Serpent? Aye there's a serpent. Out there in the waves. Can you no see it?' Joe pointed way out to sea, where the waves rolled slowly towards the western seaboard of Scotland.

Cal screwed his eyes up to focus better.

'Can you no see it?' Joe asked again, but this time with a hint of sarcasm in his voice. 'Ah well, there you are then. It's hiding 'neath the surface. You'll no see it 'til it creeps up on the rocks there, and then again when it rears its ugly head in Skiopageio.'

'Where?'

'Here. Skiopageio. The blow hole here.' Joe left his spot and walked up the cliff to a dark chasm in the rocks. Cal followed him, trailing the blanket behind.

'When the sea is running high, like she is now, the breakers catch on the outermost rocks and rocket in through the inlet, funnelling up here to break over the cliffs.'

He waited a while for the information to sink in. He wasn't sure if Cal understood him or not. It seemed perfectly simple to him. All his wondering and worrying about what had happened and here he had the answer right in front of him. It wasn't a freak wave. It was Skiopageio. The funnel. The force of water in the blowhole.

'Like a whale you mean,' Cal asked.

'Aye, like a whale if you like.'

They listened. The cacophonous music of water sucked in and out, the waves too small at the moment to demonstrate the phenomenon with any force.

'I don't understand. There's no sea serpent?'

'Where did you ever get that idea?'

'I can't rightly say now.'

'There's no sea serpent.' He smiled slyly. 'There's ghosts though,' and Joe stopped himself from saying more. He didn't really understand why he'd blurted it out like that, but if he'd been worried he need not have been. Cal didn't react. He seemed more concerned about the blowhole, and the way the waves washed and sucked, than anything else.

Joe stared far out to sea, willing the waves to grow fiercer.

'Do you think that's what happened to the others then?' Cal asked. He was bent almost double with the weight of the blanket around him. 'Got washed away?'

'Seems so.'

'Hmm. No sea serpent.'

'No.'

'Won't make so good a story.'

Joe frowned. A story. Was that was all this man wanted? A story?

'Oh I can give you a story alright.'

Cal glanced up, a flicker of hope in his eyes.

'I can tell you about a lighthouse keeper haunted by a phantom that demanded a sacrifice be given in blood before it would release him from its control.' Joe stuck his chin out. If this man wanted a story he had just the tale to tell.

'A phantom?'

'Aye, a phantom.'

'Here at the lighthouse?'

'Aye, at the lighthouse.'

'And did this phantom have a hand in what happened to the men?'

'Perhaps. Aye, I think so. Though Archie would tell you I was mad to say so, but what does an old man know, eh?'

Cal smiled wanly. Joe watched him grab at the straws he offered, all the time noting how the tide had grown higher, the waves more forceful.

'Go in man, you'll catch your death of cold out here, if you havenae already.'

Joe was waiting for the big wave that would surely come soon. He'd watched and waited and knew that the time was coming soon when the storm would burst with renewed violence on the little island. He didn't want this strange man here when that happened. He wanted to meet his maker alone.

Cal hesitated, then turned slowly towards the path. He tripped on his blanket and Joe caught him before he fell.

'I don't need your help,' Cal muttered. 'Just tell me about the damned phantom. If there are no sea serpents, at least indulge me with a phantom.' He struggled to free himself from Joe's grasp.

'All right. Not here though. In the warm. You go on ahead. I'll join you.'

Cal scowled.

'What are you hiding?'

'I'm no hiding anything. You're ill man. You shouldnae be here at all.'

Cal attempted to stand erect.

'I'm fine, just fine. No thanks to this damned country of yours.'

He broke out into a hacking cough that appeared to wring every last ounce of energy out of him. He turned back to face the sea and in that moment the waves Joe had been waiting for charged through the inlet and rocketed upwards. The spray caught both men off guard and Joe slid to grab hold of Cal and a rocky outcrop at one and the same time.

'Get off me,' Cal shouted through the noise.

Another wave washed in and up. The water cascaded over them cold and hard. Momentarily, Joe lost sight of Cal, then glimpsed him crawling up the rocks on all fours. He tried to make his way towards him. The third wave thundered through the rocky inlet, boomed round the cliffs, echoing hollow in Skiopageio before it shot upwards, the force immense, the steely water knife-like as it rained down on them. Cal slipped again, couldn't regain his grip on the rocks. Briefly, Joe touched the heel of Cal's boot. His hand closed round the leather and then lost it just as quickly. The spray hung heavy in the air. Joe slipped, slid, fought to keep his footing, came up hard against the railings, his mind racing. Was this what it had been like for his friends? Was this how they had died? For a split second Joe saw Cal spreadeagled on the rocks, the blanket gone. The newspaperman turned his head slowly.

'Get back to the lighthouse, man. Get back,' Joe shouted. He scrabbled towards Cal but the fourth wave came up, catching Joe just as he covered Cal's body with his own. He twisted round as the water rained down, pushing Cal roughly up towards higher ground.

There was almost no point in speaking at all, but he yelled: 'Save yourself,' to Cal and briefly noted the newspaperman slithering along his belly to the trackway.

Then the fifth wave hit and Joe was ready for it. He stood as best he could, stretching his arms out, face elated. At last. Death never felt so sweet. So cold. The wave died and Joe was still standing on the rocky prominence above the inlet. He glanced round. Cal was nowhere to be seen. The sea, still roaring defiance, had abated somewhat. The wind turned, the storm was already passing. A strange calmness came over Joe – as if a weight had been lifted from his shoulders.

'Joe. Joe. Where are you?' Archie's voice burst through the cacophony of the receding storm. The old man appeared way off on higher ground.

'Here. I'm here.'

'Are you alright, laddie?'

'Aye. Have you seen that barm pot that was wi me? He should be halfway back to the lighthouse by now. He's no well, that man.'

Archie stumbled down the track, taking care to mind his footing on the wet rocks.

'He's no back there.'

'Are you sure?'

'Aye. I was watching from the window. When the storm came in I put my oilskin on to come and find you, but I had to wait until it passed a wee bit.'

'I'm fine.'

'Aye, I can see that now. But where's that madman gone?'

Joe blinked. He didn't want to think about it. Skiopageio. Out to sea a blanket rode the fading waves.

The serpent.
The phantom.
An obsession.

The two men watched the blanket warp in the swell. Joe fingered the stone in his pocket. Drew it forth. Looked at it and then lobbed it into the sea.

'He'll wash up somewhere. Men like that always do.'

'Aye,' replied Archie. 'They do that.'

Original Report by Superintendent Muirhead

8th January 1901

On receipt of Captain Harvie's telegram of 26th December 1900, reporting on the three keepers at the Flannan Islands, James Ducat, Principal, Thomas Marshall, second Assistant and Donald Macarthur, Occasional Keeper (doing duty for William Ross, first Assistant on sick leave), had disappeared, that they must have been blown over cliffs or drowned I made the following arrangements with the Secretary for the temporary working of the station.

James Ferrier, Principal Keeper was sent from Stornoway Lighthouse to Tiumpanhead Lighthouse and John Milne, Principal Keeper at Tiumpanhead was sent to take temporary charge at Flannan Islands. Donald Jack, the Second Assistant Storekeeper was also dispatched to Flannan Islands, the intention being that these two men along with Joseph Moore, the third Assistant at Flannan Islands who was ashore when the accident took place, should take duty pending permanent arrangements being made. I also proceeded to Flannan Islands where I was landed along with Milne and Jack early on the 29th after satisfying myself that everything connected with the lighthouse was in good order and that the men landed would be able to maintain the light, I proceeded to ascertain, if possible, the cause of the disaster and also took statements from Captain Harvie and Mr Macormick the second mate of the Hesperus, Joseph Moore, third Assistant Keeper, Flannan Islands and Alan Macdonald, Buoymaster, and the following is the result of my investigations.

The Hesperus arrived at Flannan Islands for the purpose of making the ordinary relief about noon on Wednesday 26th December and, as neither signal was shown, nor any of the usual preparations for landing made, Captain Harvie blew both the steamer whistle and the siren to call the attention of the keepers. As this had no effect, he fired a rocket which also affected no response and a boat was lowered and sent ashore to the east landing with Joseph Moore, Assistant Keeper. When the boat reached the landing, there being still no sign of the keepers the boat was backed into the landing and with some difficulty Moore managed to jump ashore. When he went up to the station he found the entrance gate and outside doors closed, the clock stopped, no fire lit. He looked into the bedrooms and found the beds empty. He became alarmed at this and ran down to the boat and informed Mr Macormick, the Second Mate, that the keepers were missing. Macormick and one of the seamen managed to jump ashore and with Moore made a thorough search of the station but could discover nothing. They then returned to the ship and informed Captain Harvie. He told Moore he would have to return to the Isles to keep the light going pending instructions and called for volunteers from his crew to assist in this. He met with a ready response and two seamen, Lamont and Campbell, were selected, and Mr Macdonald the Buoymaster who was on board offered his services, which were accepted. Moore, Macdonald and these two seamen were left in charge of the light while Captain Harvie returned to Breascleit and telegrammed an account of the disaster to the Secretary.

The men left on the island made a thorough search in the first place of the station and found that the last entry on the slate had been made by Mr Ducat, the Principal Keeper on the morning of Saturday 15th December. The lamp was trimmed, the oil fountains and canteens were filled up and the lens and machinery clean which proved that the work of the forenoon of the 15th had been completed. The pots and pans in the kitchen had been cleaned which showed that the man who had been acting as cook had completed his work, which goes to prove that the men disappeared on the afternoon of Saturday 15th December. This is borne out by information which was received after the news of the disaster had been published. Captain Holman has passed the Flannans in the steamer Archtor at midnight on the 15th ulto, could not observe the light, though from the condition of the weather and his position he felt satisfied that he should have seen it.

On the Thursday and Friday the men made a thorough search over and round the island. I went over the ground with them on the Saturday. Everything at the east landing place was in order and the ropes that should have been coiled and stored there on the completion of the relief on the 7th were all in their places, and the lighthouse buildings and everything at the station was in order. The traces of the severity of the weather were however to be found in the west landing place. Owing to the amount of the sea I could not get down to the west landing place but I got down to the crane platform, about 70 feet above sea level. The crane originally erected on this platform was washed away during last winter and the crane that was put up there in the summer was found to be unharmed, the jib lowered and secured on the rocks and the canvas covering and the wire rope on the barrel securely lashed round it. There was no evidence that the men had been doing anything at the crane. The mooring ropes, landing ropes, derrick landing ropes and crane handles and also a wooden box in which they were kept and which was secured in a crevice in the rocks 70 feet up the tramway from the terminus and about 40 feet higher than the crane platform, or 110 feet in all above the sea level had been washed away and the ropes strewn in the crevices of the rock near the crane platform and entangled along the crane legs but they were all coiled up, no single coil being found unfastened. The iron railings around the crane platform from the terminus of the tramway to the concrete steps up from the west landing were displaced and twisted. A large block of stone weighing upwards of twenty cwt had been dislodged from its position higher up and carried down and left on the concrete path leading from the terminus of the tramway to the top of the steps. The lifebuoy fastened to the railings along this path, to be used in case of emergency, had disappeared. I thought at first it had been removed for the purpose of being used, but on examining the ropes by which it was fastened I found that they had not been touched and as pieces of canvas were adhered to the ropes, it was evident that the force of the sea pouring through the railings had even at this great height, 110 feet above sea level, torn away the lifebuoy off the ropes.

When the accident occurred Ducat was wearing seaboots and waterproof. Marshall, seaboots and oilskins. As Moore assures me that the men wore only those articles when going down to the landings, they must have intended, when they left the station, to go down to the landing or the proximity of it. After carefully examining the place, the railings, ropes etc… and weighing up all the evidence which I could secure, I am of the opinion that the most likely explanation of the disappearance of the men is that they had all gone down in the afternoon of Saturday 15th December to a proximity of the west landing to secure the box with the mooring ropes etc… and that an unexpectedly large roller had come up on the island. A large body of water coming up higher than where they were and coming down, swept them *away with a resistless force. I considered and discussed the possibility of men being blown away by the wind but as the wind was westerly I am of the opinion, notwithstanding its great force, that the more probable explanation is that they had been washed away, as had the wind caught them it would, from its direction, have blown them up the island and I feel certain that they would have been able to throw themselves down before they reached the summit or brow of the island.*

On the conclusion of my enquiry on Saturday I returned to Breascleit, wired the result of my investigation to the Secretary and called upon the widows of James Ducat, Principal Keeper, and Donald Macarthur, the Occasional Keeper. I may state that Moore was naturally very much upset by the unfortunate occurrence and appeared very nervous. I left Archie Lamont, Seaman on the island, to go to the lightroom and keep Moore company when on watch for a week or two. If this nervousness does not leave Moore, he will require to be transferred, but I am reluctant to recommend this as I would desire to have one man at least who knows the work of the station.

The Commissioners appointed Roderick Mackenzie, game-keeper, Uig, near Mevaig to look out daily for signals that might be shown from the rock and to note each night whether the light was seen or not. As it was evident that the light had not been lit from the 15th to the 26th December I resolved to see him on Sunday morning to ascertain what he had to say on the subject. He was away from home, but I found his two sons, aged 18 and 16, two most intelligent lads of the gamekeeper class, who actually perform the duties of looking out for the signal and I had a conversation with them on the matter, and I also examined the Return Book. From the December return I saw the tower itself was not seen, even with the assistance of a powerful telescope between the 7th and the 29th December. The light was however seen on the 7th December but was not seen on the 8th, 9th, 10th or 11th. It was seen on the 12th but was not seen again until the 26th, the night it was lit by Moore. Mackenzie stated, and I have since verified this, that the light can some times not been seen for four or five consecutive nights but he was beginning to be anxious at not seeing it for such a long period and had, for two nights, prior to its reappearance been getting the assistance of the natives to see if it could be discerned. Had a lookout been kept by an ordinary lighthousekeepers as at Earraid from Dubh Artach,

I believe it would have struck the man ashore at an earlier period that something was amiss, and while this would not have prevented the lamentable occurrence taking place it would have enabled steps to have been taken to have the light re-lit at an earlier date. I would recommend that the Signalman should be instructed that in future, should he fail to observe the light when in his opinion, looking to the state of the atmosphere it should be seen, he should be instructed to intimate this to the Secretary, where the propriety of taking the appropriate steps could be considered.

I may explain that the signals are shown from Flannan Islands by displaying balls or discs each side of the tower on poles projecting out from the Lighthouse balcony, the signals being differentiated by one or more discs being shown on the different sides of the tower. When at the Flannan Islands so lately as the 7th December last I had a conversation with the late Mr Ducat regarding the signals and he stated that he wished it may be necessary to hoist one of the signals just to ascertain how soon it would be seen on shore and how soon it would be acted upon. At that time I took note to consider the propriety of having a daily signal that all was well – signals and other present system being only exhibited when assistance was required. But after careful consideration on the matter and discussing it with the officials competent to offer an opinion on the subject I arrived at the conclusion that it would not be advisable to have such a signal as owing to the distance between the Island and the shore, and to the frequency of haze on the top of the Island it would often been unseen for such a duration of time as to cause alarm especially on the part of the Keepers' wives and families and I would point out that no daily signals could have been seen between the 7th and 29th December. An 'all well' signal could have been of no use on this occasion. The question had been raised as to how we would have been situated had wireless telegraphy been instituted, but had we failed to establish communication for some days I should have concluded that something had gone wrong with the signalling apparatus and the last thing that would have occurred to me was that all three men would have disappeared.

In conclusion, I would desire to record my deep regret at such a disaster occurring to Keepers in this Service. I knew Ducat and Marshall intimately and Macarthur, the Occasional, well. They were selected on my recommendation on the lighting of such an important station as the Flannan Islands, and as it was always my endeavour to secure the best men possible for the establishment of a station, as the success and contentment at a station depends largely on the Keepers present in its installation, this in itself is an indication that the Board have lost two of its most efficient Keepers and a competent Occasional. I was with the Keepers for more than a month during the summer of 1899 when everyone worked hard to secure the early lighting of the station before winter and working along with them, I appreciated the manner in which they performed their work. I visited the Flannan Isles when the relief was made so lately as the 7th December, and I have the melancholy recollection that I was the last person to shake hands with them when I bid them adieu.

*

From William Ross to NLB

Sir

In reply to your letter of the 10th inst. requesting me to give all the information I can obtain regarding to Mrs Macarthur, widow of the late Occasional Keeper. I beg to say that Mrs Macarthur is 32 years of age with two of her family; a boy age ten and a girl age seven years both at school. She came here seven years ago with her late husband when he got his discharge from the Royal Engineers, afterwards being five years in the reserve. He was a native of Breascleit and she was born and brought up in Gravesend, England and can get nothing to do here to earn a livelihood. If she had the means to pay her way she would go to her native place where she has friends and might find something to do for herself.

I am Sir, you obedient servant
William Ross

*

Original Memo by Robert Muirhead January 1901

In my report of the 8th inst. on the Flannan Isles disaster I stated that Moore, Assistant Keeper, was very much upset by the unfortunate circumstances, and in a high state of nervousness. When on the Flannan Islands on the 29th ulto Moore informed me that he could not remain at that station, but on my pointing out to him the great disadvantage of having all the staff new men, he agreed to continue doing duty in the meantime in the hope that his nervousness would wear off. I stated at the same time that under the circumstances I felt assured that the Commissioner would not insist on his being kept there should he consider it be necessary to be transferred. Moore has written me requesting a transfer but agreeing to remain at the Flannans until the new men are up to the work of the station. I do not consider it advisable to retain him on the Flannans, either in his own interests or that of the station. I would recommend that A Maclachlan of Stourhead and he exchange places and would suggest that transfer.

*

15th January 1901

Transfer to be made on the 22nd February, by which time the new men will be into the work of the station.

*

Letter for the Secretary Northern Lighthouse Board, Commissioners

Dear Sir

With reference to the most regrettable catastrophe at the Flannan Isles, Captain Holman of the SS Archtor of Philadelphia reported to us on his arrival here on the 18th inst. that he did not observe the Flannan light in passing thereabout at midnight on the 15th inst. The night was stormy but clear. This seems to indicate that the accident took place on the 15th inst. or prior thereto.

We should have brought this matter under your notice previously but having been so much occupied by the accident to this steamer and other affairs the matter escaped our memory.

Yours faithfully
Henderson and Mackintosh.

APPENDIX

❧

*A*ll the documents appearing in this novel are copies of the original Northern Lighthouse Board records, now held in the National Archives of Scotland in Edinburgh.

This is a true story, but as with all history certain facts can only be surmised. Joseph Moore did find the lighthouse abandoned when he landed on that fateful day on 26th December 1900. His report, that of Superintendent Muirhead, and Muirhead's later note, all testify to Joe's fragile state of mind. Joseph Moore never married and left no close relatives.

Most of the characters in this novel really did exist. The lighthouse keepers' wives – Mary Ducat, and Annie Macarthur, their children, all the keepers named herein, Superintendent Muirhead, Secretary Murdoch of the NLB, Captain Harvie and the sailors on *Hesperus*, Captain Holman of the tramp steamer *Archtor*, and the Mackenzies were all real people.

Their characters have been embellished, but I have attempted to stay as close to the facts as possible.

The Principal Keeper's wife, Mary Ducat, only survived her late husband by another two years. She died of breast cancer and relatives brought Annabella and the other Ducat children up. Later they set up a draper's in Edinburgh. None of the children ever married. Annie Macarthur became a district nurse. She was remembered as having a strange 'Cockney Gaelic'. Joseph Moore is thought by Breascleit local historian Merrilyn Macaulay to have 'Gaelge', or Irish Gaelic, as he hailed originally from Belfast by way of Kirkcaldy, Fife. She goes on to conjecture that a Gaelic-speaking child in Belfast named Joseph was surely also a Catholic. This might be something that he would keep quiet on an island beset at the time by Protestant infighting. However, there is no evidence to prove one way or the other whether Joe was a Catholic or not. I think that he might simply have picked Gaelic up from the local population, although the lighthouse keepers often kept themselves to themselves while on shore.

As to Callum Robinson – he was the phantom. He never existed at all save in my imagination and in your dreams.